The Wizard of Fire

M.J. Fitzmaurice

The Wizard of Fire – 2nd edition Copyright © 2023 by M.J. Fitzmaurice

All rights reserved.

No portion of this book may be reproduced in any form without written permission from the publisher or author, except as permitted by U.S. copyright law.

Contents

1. The Strange Voice — 1
2. The Trial — 8
3. Stumbling in the Dark — 15
4. A Storm, A Bridge, and a Troll — 22
5. Encounter — 28
6. The Wolf Pack — 35
7. Vision and Seizure — 42
8. The Mine Slaves — 49
9. The Prisoners — 56
10. Finding Chortnel — 63
11. The King and I — 70
12. Finding Sam — 77
13. Emancipation — 84
14. Finding the Way — 91
15. The End of a Culture — 98
16. Reunited — 106
17. The Aftermath — 114

18.	The Factions	121
19.	King Ruuc	129
20.	Power's Resolution	136
21.	A Pirate Encounter	143
22.	A New Arrival	150
23.	A Pirate's Life	158
24.	The Sailing Ship	166
25.	Jade Ayu	174
26.	Disputed Property	181
27.	The Escape Plan	188
28.	Mr. Sparks is not Happy	196
29.	Harbortown	203
30.	The Pirate Problems	211
31.	The Pirate Solution	219
32.	The Departure	227

Chapter One

The Strange Voice

I kick at the rocks on the gravel pathway. "We're going to shake people up tonight, aren't we, Sam?" My pack's light on my back. It holds only a few gourds of water after a nearly two-week trek, part of what my mother calls Hawk's Wandering.

Samuel Pettifog—I named him after my favorite Bard—looks at me sideways but doesn't speak. He sniffs the side of the road, finding something interesting for a moment, then runs to catch back up to me.

Samuel is a big black hound with curly hair, bright eyes, and an exuberance for life that would irritate the heck out of me if Sam was human. Ma gave him to me on my twelfth birthday. Sam is my best friend in the entire world. There is nothing we would not do for each other.

A breeze moves around me. It's the season of storms now, and rain will start soon. The thunder and lightning passing over Hovel, my village, usually lasts off and on for three months.

I'm thinking of my discovery. It's something so mind-blowing that even now I can't wrap my head all the way around it. There is a boundary of the world— and it has a hole in it! Think of it: me, Hawk Archer is about to announce to the entire village that they had been wrong for... well, forever, I guess.

There is a celebration tonight for 100,000 years. The scribes and preachers have the records, some are in tatters. No one really knows how we got here under the clouds, under the light but they all agree when it started, when the world was created.

The light coming through the clouds begins to dim, signaling the start of another day. Soon, the dim light will be just enough to allow a person to find their way home to bed. Then that will fade, and there will be barely enough light to find a way in the darkness.

There are stories that the end of the world will happen. Other stories claim The Light itself will appear out of the clouds and unite all the countries of the world, appearing in each town and village that has kept the records.

Of course, stories of the beginning are more plentiful than the clouds—how it came to be, why we were put here, and who made it.

Some of those stories tell of a world beyond the world. Those stories are told in hushed privacy where the clergy can't hear and punish you for sharing blasphemy.

I don't care about the stories. Shoving my hair behind my ears, I trudge on. I can see the tower at the center of town now. Stretched across it is a burlap banner proclaiming the celebration.

"Sixty seconds to a minute, sixty minutes to an hour, twenty-four hours in a day." The song taught to all of us from the time we could talk pops into my head. The months are named—no one knows for sure why, but there are stories. People always have stories.

"Sam, why do you think people make things up? Like they have to have a reason for everything, right?" I bend a little to reach the dog's head and ruffle the fur there. "People would be better off if they were more like dogs. Taking life one moment at a time and enjoying it without trying to explain it all."

I walk into town. There is a crowd around the village center. Preacher's there, standing next to my mother.

I ask, "Sam, why do you think he wears black all the time? I mean if he's the representative of Light, then shouldn't he be wearing white?" Sam takes my words as he always does; he ignores them. Unless he hears his name or food mentioned, Sam has no interest in conversation. He sniffs the air, then he whines.

I say, "Smelling the sausage and steaks, are you?" I smell them as well. My stomach growl surprises me. I have not thought of being hungry since discovering the hole in the world. Sam and I jogged all the way back to town, three nights and days, only resting when I could go no further.

Now I am here, and as the village, and the world, move towards the new year and the new epoch. I think that's what Preacher calls it, a new epoch. I want to talk to my mother, Salient Archer, before the daylight departs and people start finding their way home in the twilight.

Ma is a tall dark-haired woman, and anyone seeing her and I together know we are related. She is dressed in deep red and blue, her skirt down to her ankles and matching the print of her kerchief.

Ma says, "Finally back, Hawk? I was getting ready to send a search party out."

I reply, "Ma, I found something strange to the west. A boundary, a wall that blocks passage out of the world. Plus, old, rusted rails leading into a hole in the wall!"

Salient touches her forehead and then her lips. "You went to the end of the earth? You know that is forbidden."

I shrug. "I'm alive, Ma. There's no monsters or sickness out there. I touched the wall where it sinks into the earth."

I can see the Preacher is listening, so I place a hand on Ma's shoulder—I'm taller than she is now—and I lead her away, out of the black-clad clergyman's hearing. "Ma, there's a tunnel where those tracks go into the side of a mountain, leading somewhere outside here."

Salient's face goes scarlet. "You listen to me, Hawk Archer. You stay away from that place. Decent people don't go wandering around in the forbidden areas. You are going to ruin everything. Jobe expected you two days ago to start your apprenticeship."

"Ma, I told you, I'm not going to be a darn tinker."

Ma blinks and tears form in her eyes.

I say, "Ma, don't do that. Please don't cry."

"I can be thankful your blessed father can't see you like this. Shirking work, wandering off all the time. I just hope the Everafter has him too distracted to look down and see you like this."

I want to yell, but I don't want a scene. One of my biggest flaws is totally misunderstanding what people think of things. I've always been the outsider, always questioning what everyone else takes for granted. What I see as perfectly reasonable, others always get offended by or take exception to.

Up to this very moment, I had buried the idea I had as soon as I saw that tunnel. Now, I let the idea fully form. I am going to leave Hovel. Even though there are tears in Ma's eyes, I know I'm right. I love her, but I am done being manipulated by her, Preacher, and Jobe.

"Ma, I'm going away."

Ma's eyes go wide with fear and surprise. At least I think that's what it is. Just then, Dahlia interrupts us.

"Everything okay, Ms. Archer?" Dahlia's my age, and I always feel pulled to her when we run into each other. She has hair as dark as mine, skin a couple of shades lighter, and a smile that shines bright enough to light up the dark hours.

Ma shakes her head. "No, nothing is okay. My son wants to leave me." She turns and walks off without another word. Then our village scribe, Hobsin, goes to the podium. There are no blaring trumpets or shaking ground. The clouds don't part or light up bright as day. "Good people of Hovel!" Hobsin raises his arms and looks out over the crowd as the light in the clouds dims, starting a new day. He looks up into the clouds and then back at the assembly, "Our 100,000 year of existence is now official!"

The village is quiet for a few seconds, and cheers erupt. The Sandovals are hugging. The Overjoys dance and twirl. I don't understand what the fuss is about. It's just a stupid number.

I say, "So much for the end of the earth."

Dahlia touches her head and lips. "You shouldn't joke about such things, Hawk. Preacher will hear about it."

I shrug. "The Light take him. I don't care. This town, all the towns around us, and everyone I know keeps telling me what I can and cannot say. I'm done, Dahlia. I'm leaving."

Dahlia frowns. "What? Leaving where? Are you going to move to another town?"

I grin at her. "Better. I found a way out of the dome, off the earth. I'm going to go find where it leads."

Dahlia has a confused look, and she touches her head and lips again in the gesture to ward off evil and blasphemy. "There's no hole in the boundary of the world. There's nothing beyond it. You know that."

As she talks, I hear a humming sound. I look up at the clouds and the light is acting strange. I blink and look up again. The light is brighter and then dims rapidly. It's flashing and making me dizzy, making me blink. I look at Dahlia, I feel disoriented and confused. She says something but I can't hear it. It's as if she is talking underwater.

I look around. The noise of the crowd is muted as well. The Preacher is standing with some of the elders, looking up at the clock. The scene is blurry, and I blink, then shake my head, but it doesn't change. I hear a whisper, loud inside my head, "Come." I see a picture of the hole I'd found. Then the lights stop blinking.

I look at Dahlia. "Did you hear that?"

Dahlia frowns at me. "Hear what?"

I hear her normal voice. I look back at the people standing around the bandstand. They are just as they always are.

I realize my mouth is open, so shut it. The voice is gone, the blurred vision with it.

I say, "I dunno, I thought I heard a voice, and everything got blurry for a moment."

Dahlia looks at me funny and edges away. "I need to go find my folks. Talk to you later, Hawk." Her smile is definitely telling me I'm an imbecile. The light dims. I look up to see that the clouds are growing grey, turning deep shades towards black.

I decide I need to find my mother, to explain to her. I look over the crowd trying to find her. I spot her with the tallest person who lives in Hovel. She's talking to Preacher. My guts squeeze, but I pucker up and decide I might as well get this over with.

I walk up to Ma. "Ma, please, we need to talk."

Preacher says sternly, "Hawk, your mother tells me you went out into the forbidden areas."

I sigh but decide to ignore the man in black. "Ma, please, I really need to talk to you."

Ma turns to me, wiping tears from her eyes with a black hanky. I think, man this guy has black handkerchiefs even.

Ma looks at me, and her eyes hold both pity and accusation. No one does that look better than Ma.

"I have no son," she says. "He abandoned me, left me all alone, and now I have nothing." Then she loses the power of speech in her sobs. The Preacher puts an arm around her, and while he comforts my mother, he glares at me.

I feel the steel of the Preacher's gaze trying to penetrate my heart, and then the world goes soft again. Noises seem filtered through water, and my eyesight is blurry. The voice whispers loud in my head again. "COME," it says, and again I see a picture of the hole in the boundary wall.

I shake my head, trying to clear it. I see that Preacher is looking at me like he is waiting for an answer to some question I hadn't heard.

I say to him, "Look, you and I have never seen things the same way. I am just not cut out to be one of your sheep, Preacher. You can look down that long nose of yours all you want, but what can you do about it? Lock me in the jail hut?"

Ten minutes later I contemplate why I would give the Preacher ideas like that. The goons, who answer to Preacher, shove me into the jail hut and slam the door closed. One of them shoves the bar through the locking ring. I hear whining on the other side of the door.

I say to Samuel, "You could have at least tried to slobber on them, slow them down a bit."

Samuel lies in front of the door, groaning softly. He sets his head on his paws, stares up at me and blinks his sad soulful eyes. That's when the world goes completely dark.

Chapter Two

The Trial

I figure it's night, so I lay down on the bunk. I contemplate my fate and what Preacher might do to me. I will suggest to him that I be banished. That will work for both of us, won't it?

I drift off. When I wake, I open my eyes, but I can't see anything. I blink but it's still dark. I must have woken early as it is pitch black in the cell. I sit up and rub my eyes. I really have to pee but I'm not sure where the slop bucket is. By its smell, I know it's somewhere across the room by the window.

I move in that direction, feeling on the ground slowly until my toe touches something. I reach down and pick up the bucket. It really stinks, but I hold my breath and let go.

After relieving myself, I move to the corner and set the bucket down where I know I can find it again if, Light forbid, I need it before it gets light. Through the window, I can hear the sound of people talking in strained voices. Standing on the tips of my toes, I just manage to see out of the barred window.

Something is wrong. People are pointing up at the clouds and the distress is obvious on their faces, in their speech. Before I can take that thought further, Samuel yelps and then someone bangs on the door's lock mechanism.

I can see torchlight through the bars on the door. The door opens, and Portus, one of the goons who brought me here, steps in, grinning at me.

"Pick up your bucket and come with me." Portus holds the door open and gestures. I reached into the corner, grab the slop bucket, thinking I might pay the big guy back for kicking Samuel, but instead I take it outside and dump it in the street like a normal person.

I set the bucket down by the door, then Portus grabs me and ties my hands. He's a big guy, but I want him to know I'm not intimidated.

I say, "You hurt my dog again and I'll kill you."

He just laughs and shoves me toward the commons. I stumble a few times, as the light coming from a bonfire at the town center isn't enough to show the path we are walking on.

Portus walks me to the center, where Preacher is sitting behind a rough wooden table. On either side is a church elder. One is Farns Bentley, who is always decent to me. Farns never shows much in the way of temper, and I think he might be my ally here.

On the other side of Preacher sits Stigs Blaat. Now, Stigs is a piece of work. The kind of person to laugh if you got your leg broke or had a beehive fall on your head. Stigs smiles at me, but it's like he is seeing a fat pork chop sizzling in a frying pan.

Portus shoves me towards the table. There are candles placed all around, a flickering light on the three judges. It's all very eerie.

I wonder if maybe the night sky not being lit up is more than a coincidence. Maybe who—or what—put the visions in my head caused the lights to go out, though I can't think of a reason for doing so. If they want me to go to the hole in the boundary, then shutting down the lights isn't very helpful.

Preacher raises his long nose in the air and says in a voice loud enough that everyone around the bandstand can hear, "What do you have to say for yourself, Hawk Archer?"

I looked around for Ma, but she isn't here. Probably ill from the prospect of his punishment, at least that's what I'm telling myself.

I turn back and say, "Preacher, there's a boundary hidden by the clouds. There's a wall out there and it has a hole in it."

Preacher bangs his hammer on a wrought iron anvil. Each blow makes my ears ring, making any conversation impossible. The ringing subsides and he looks at me. In a loud angry voice, he says, "You have caused the Light to depart from Earth. Your abomination has brought ruin to us. What do you have to say about that?"

I blink. I guess I probably should have seen this coming. After all, I was just speculating about the possible connection. Why wouldn't everyone else in Hovel wonder the same thing?

Stigs points a fat piggy finger at me and says, "You must be punished. We must show the Light we are faithful. You must burn!"

I gulp audibly. The bonfire? They aren't really considering throwing me in there. I stammer a bit, then say, "Listen, you can just banish me, okay? That should be good enough for the Light, right? I mean, the Light is benevolent, isn't it? You all can even shun me on my way out, turn your backs and all that. What do you say, Preacher? There's no need to burn me, is there?"

Preacher leans forward. "So you admit to being the cause of the darkness, Hawk Archer?"

Uh oh, did I just get outmaneuvered? I shake my head. "Look, I don't know why the Light went away. Really, I don't. I'm just a small village idiot who likes to wander around and discover things. The Light doesn't care about people like me, right? I'm just a nuisance. Let me go, and I promise I will never come back. That should be enough for the Light, don't you think, Preacher?" I give him a weak laugh.

My stomach growls. They didn't feed me last night or this morning. You'd think if they were planning to burn a guy, they might at least feed him first. I looked around for Samuel. He's sitting at the bottom of the stairs, a plate of meat leavings in front of him, half devoured. Well, at least someone was kind to my dog.

Preacher leans left and whispers to Stig, nods at the reply, and then leans right, repeating the process with Farns. He nods, then looks at me.

Just then, another vision strikes. This time the feeling that everyone is underwater is powerful. The flickering from the candles and the bonfire seems three times faster than normal, and I can't hear what Preacher is telling me.

"Come." Whoever is putting this thought into my head is louder this time—still a whisper, but more like someone straining to speak loudly while maintaining the appearance of a whisper. The vision of the hole in the wall I'd found is huge this time. In the vision, I'm standing under the hole, and I can see weeds and boulders covering rusted metal tracks that lead inside.

Then I blink and realize I'm on the floor and Portus is poking me.

"Get up!" He says, not very kindly. He pokes me again in the back with a huge finger, and this time I flinch.

I stand shakily. "Sorry, I guess I'm a little weak. I haven't eaten in a long time and, well, what did you say, Preacher?"

Preacher shakes his head and waves a hand at me. "Take him back to the jail hut, Portus. See that he gets a meal while we deliberate what to do with him."

Portus grabs me and drags me away. Samuel trots after us, whining a bit but not doing anything to save me. I wonder if I should've trained him to attack or something. Of course, I have no idea how you train a dog to do that.

Portus yanks me along, making me stumble. He has a handful of my jerkin in his grasp, so I don't fall, just kind of stumble along.

"Portus, what did Preacher say? When I fainted, I mean. What was he saying was going to happen to me?"

Portus grins. "They gonna burn you. Farns probably made them discuss it first, but Preacher and Stig want to see you cook, Archer."

I don't know what to say to that. I try to think of ways to escape.

I take some small, very small, consolation that once I'd been made crispy and black, the Light will still be gone. That will show them, make them sorry for doing this to me. Of course, it would be better if they come to their senses before that, but this is Hovel after all. They all follow the Preacher and the council elders.

Portus kicks me in the behind, and I sprawl to the ground, hitting a pebble with my nose. It hurts. I can feel blood dripping.

Once we reach the jail hut, Portus holds me with one hand and opens the door with the other. He shoves me inside and throws the bucket in after me. It hits me in the head and bounces into a corner as he slams the door shut.

"Ow!" I yelp. "Light take you, Portus!"

"Enjoy yourself Archer. Your last meal will be here in a bit." I hear him stroll away. I work my hands out of the rope, then I get busy. I just about finish inspecting the entire room when there is a knock on the door.

The door creaks open. A flickering torch shows the faces of Dahlia and her father. He looks grim. He's holding a covered dish. He nods to Dahlia, who glances at me before standing back, her eyes on the floor.

Mr. Evens says, "Here ya go. My wife made you steak and potatoes, and there's fresh squash in there with a little butter."

I take the dish. "Thank you, Mr. Evens, Dahlia."

He gives me a harsh look. "Probably more than you deserve considering what you done, but even a condemned man ought to have a last meal."

I don't know what to say to that, so I just say, "Yes sir. Thank you again. Thank you, Dahlia."

Dahlia says, "Goodbye Hawk". She turns and walks away. Mr. Evens nods to me, shuts the door and locks it.

I pull the cloth off the plate of food. There's no knife or spoon. Probably worried I'll dig myself out of the hut. I pick up the steak and bite in. It's good. I chew and then take another bite. Now that my hunger has been awakened, it doesn't seem to matter I am going to die in a few hours.

When I finish the plate, I set it down by the door. Then it occurs to me that maybe I can dig under the hut. I grab the plate and begin scooping dirt away from the wall. Then I realize I'm digging next to the door, not a smart move when Portus or one of his thug friends will be along to guard me soon. I move over by the window and started digging.

I don't know how long I dig. Eventually, hands and fingers numb with the effort, I have a hole big enough for Samuel to climb in. He whines and licks my face while I hug him.

I tell him, "Okay that's enough. We need to make this hole big enough for me to crawl out of." I feel Sam go through the hole and start digging from the other side.

When it's deep enough, I toss the plate, get down on all fours, and try to get through. It isn't working, then I realize I might be able to crawl out on my back. I reverse and start again. I scrape something with my belly on the way and grit my teeth so as not to scream.

I make it out, dust myself off, hug Samuel one more time, and go around to the door to get my pack. I pick it up just as I hear voices.

"They couldn't wait until morning. They really want to do this in the middle of the night?"

I recognize Portus answering, "It's nighttime all the time now, dimwit. Just open the door."

I scoot around back and take off before they discover I'm gone.

Chapter Three

Stumbling in the Dark

I guess I hadn't really thought this through. I stumble around in the dark, heading in what I think is a westerly direction, keeping the red glow of the town's torches and fires behind me. As I stumble, I trip over a rock, and then step on Samuel's paw, making him yip. Being the good friend he is, he immediately forgives me and licks my face while I feel his paw for any damage.

The glow disappears, and I am alone in a deep blackness. I walk slow, but I head off the edge of the road anyway. I climb back onto the path and do my best to stay in the center of it.

Then the glow of the village appears in front of me. I think this is really hopeless. How am I going to find my way once I get to the dunes? I can't stay in the right direction with a road to follow, and there is no way I am going to make it through the forests and then the sand dunes, to the fields beyond where the dome meets the ground.

I see lights moving from town coming my way. They must've decided letting me go was not as good an option as making me a burnt offering to the dome. I can avoid them, I suppose, maybe even use them to keep me going in the right direction, but that still would not solve the essential problem of having no clue what direction I am going in without some reference like the lights or the road.

Just then, the world goes under water for me again. Another vision. The voice in my head is hurtful and loud. "Come." The vision lasts a long time, and this time I'm going inside a tunnel, climbing boulders to make my way through it.

Before I can regain my footing and my senses, someone shouts, "Here he is! Over here!" I recognize the voice of Distlin Rute. Distlin works in the trade office overseeing the exchange of stuff coming from other villages.

I turn and start to run, but there is a big toothy grin. Portus has somehow managed to sneak around me. He says, "Got you!" His fist is coming toward my face fast, and then there is darkness.

I wake up, shake my head, and realize I can't move. They have me tied to a chair.

"He's awake, good. Let's get this over with." I recognize the voice as that of Jon Rute before I open my eyes. I blink and shake my head. This time the entire council of elders is sitting at the table. Farns, Stigs, Jon, Preacher, and Morcel Evens, Dahlia's father, all sit looking at me with grim expressions.

Preacher says, "Kind of silly of you Hawk, stumbling around in the dark."

I reply, "Was it? I mean, what would you choose? Running away in the darkness, or being burned alive?"

Preacher doesn't answer. Stigs grins, but Farns and Morcel look away.

There is the patter of rain on the covering installed over the proceedings, and though my back is to the commons, the lack of any other sound makes me wonder if anyone from the village has bothered to show up.

The clouds light up, making me blink, and then a loud crashing thunder rolls over us. Maybe someone up there is on my side. I haven't had a vision again, but I've only been awake a few minutes. I think it might be nice if a vision takes over when the fire starts eating me. Might make the pain more bearable. I can hope, right?

Stigs calls to someone I can't see. "You were generous with the pitch, I hope? We don't need the fire being extinguished by this storm."

Preacher stands and has to raise his voice to be heard over the sound of rain hitting the canvas roof. I can see the fire starting to hiss.

Preacher says, "Hawk Archer, you have been charged with blasphemy and bringing everyone in Hovel disfavor from the Light. You have been found guilty and sentenced to die by fire. Do you have any last words?"

I said, "Is Ma here?"

Preacher clears his throat. "Your mother is very distraught and being cared for. I thought it best if she didn't have to witness your punishment."

"Punishment? Killing me is a bit more than punishment. Let's be honest at least, Preacher. If I'm going to die for you, the least you can do is call it what it is. I'm to be sacrificed for your superstition, your insane belief that somehow the Light up there is alive and wants my death. Well, if there is a Light, may it banish you from its presence. The darkness take you, Preacher." I don't know where that came from, really. Normally I'm not an angry person. I guess there is just something about his smug face and long nose that irritates me, or maybe it's my impending death that makes me angry.

Preacher nods to Portus and another of the elder's goons. They untie me, then pick me up out of the chair and drag me to the edge of the bonfire. Then they re-tie my legs and my wrists.

Portus said, "I'm supposed to gag you, Hawk, but I'm going to pretend I forgot so I can listen to your pretty screams while you burn." He chuckles.

The two people tending the fire are tossing buckets of black oily pitch into it. The flames burn higher and higher. Portus and the other goon grab me and are all set to toss me in when it happens.

For me, and I'm sure it's different for everyone else who is here, the world freezes. The rain drops just hang still in the air while a white-hot bolt of lightning shoots straight at me. I can actually see it zig zagging as it gets closer.

Before it can hit me, I know what to do. I don't know where the knowledge comes from. I'd never before had a thought to bending fire or lightning, but I somehow know what to do and I do it.

I split the bolt into three pieces. One cuts the ropes holding my legs together, one cuts the ropes binding my wrists, and the third one I bend into a 'U' shape and shoot it straight back up into the air into the clouds. I know where to direct it, somehow. I can't see through the cloud cover exactly, it's more like feeling my way around the other side of them.

It works. The world unfreezes and rain hits me in the face. My arms and legs are no longer bound, and the lights are on, lighting up the entire land as far as I can see.

Everyone looks at me, mouths open, eyes wide. Farns, Jon, and Marcel get on their knees and, holding their hands together, they pray a thanksgiving to the dome, and then to me. Preacher is staring at the sky, blinking as the rain hits him in the face. The storm is moving on now and lightning strikes a kilometer away. As it moves off, the rain eases. The fire hisses, then stops sputtering. I smile, thinking an evil thought.

Before I think about what I'm doing, I make a tongue of flame shoot out of the fire and hit Stigs squarely in the crotch. He yelps and starts patting himself to put out the flames.

I tell him, "That's for kicking Samuel, you piece of dung." I spit on the ground in front of him. I realize that Sam isn't there. I look around and then whistle for him. He doesn't come, so I call for him.

Preacher says, in a rather numb voice, "Your dog is with your mother."

I nod and look at Preacher. I suppose I should say something profound and meaningful. Something to make him shake in his boots and get on his knees to pray like the others, but I guess I'm not cut out to be a prophet, a god, or whatever.

I say, "Thanks Preacher. I'm going to leave now. I suggest none of you follow me. You understand me, right?"

Preacher nods. "Sure, Hawk. You go on now. No one is going to try to stop you."

I nod and walk away towards my house. It will be my house no longer after today. But I need to get Sam and gather up a few things before leaving.

When I reach home, Ms. Evens and Dahlia are there. They look at me like I am a ghost.

My mother faints. Ms. Evens says, "Hawk. You're not dead."

I bite my tongue, not wanting to let loose the biting angry sarcasm I felt. I say, "Nope, I'm very much alive, and I'd like to talk with my mother alone if you don't mind, please. I'm going to be leaving now, and I want to say goodbye first."

Dahlia said, "Hawk, I'm sorry about all this. I ..."

I held up a hand. "No apologies necessary. You did what all the village did. I'm not holding it against anyone. So, if you and your mother could just go, I need to talk to Ma before I leave. I'd really appreciate it."

I do my best to sound reasonable, but I can't help the anger I feel for them wanting me dead, or at the least not caring enough to try and prevent the elders from burning me alive.

Dahlia doesn't look at me after that. She just gets up, and taking her mother's hand, she walks them both out and closes the door.

I squat next to Ma and pat her cheek. "Ma, wake up. It's me, Hawk. Wake up, Ma."

She groans and blinks when she sees me. She hugs me to her before I can do anything. She says, "Oh Hawk, I couldn't stop them. I didn't want you dead, but I couldn't stop them. I'm so glad you're alive. But how...?" She pulls back and looks at me, waiting for an answer.

I say, "Ma, I'm leaving." I don't want to get into the whole fire and lightning thing. She'll hear about it soon enough. "I'm going to that hole I found, and I'm going to find out what's beyond it."

She hugs me. "I'm so sorry, Hawk. I'm sorry I'm not a better mother. I'm sorry I couldn't protect you."

"Ma, it's okay. You have to live here." I don't see how she could live with herself knowing she did nothing while her son was being murdered, but this was the last time I'd ever see her most likely. I don't want to leave angry. I pull her arms away. "I'm going to pack some things and get going."

She stands. "I'll help you pack."

When I'm ready, I face my mother, trying to etch the sight of her face into my memory. She has a lot of faults, this woman, but she took care of me. Made sure I was fed and clothed, and in her way, tried to steer me towards a better life.

"I love you, Ma."

She has tears in her eyes. "You come back and see me, Hawk. You come back, you here? You promise your mother this isn't the last time I'll see my boy."

What can I do? I give her my promise and kiss her cheek. Then I whistle for Sam and head out towards the west. I never look back.

Chapter Four

A Storm, A Bridge, and a Troll

My anger recedes as I walk. I've always loved to walk. I think it has to do with getting away from the village, from those people who always seemed foreign to me somehow. My head is clear and the clouds are white, not the gray of being full of rain. I breathe in the scents of flowers, hear the humming of annoying insects.

I try to summon up fire, but it isn't working. I think I can only call it when I'm in serious danger. Maybe when someone close to me is. I look at Samuel with his tongue hanging out, bounding off the road and into the grasslands on the outskirts of the village. He stops every once in a while when he finds an interesting scent, gets it all into his nose, then bounds away again.

If anyone tries to hurt Samuel, I think I can call down the lightning.

The light dims, and dark clouds pass over me. I look back at the village and see there is heavy rain falling there. I don't hear the thunder, but I see a lightning strike. I hope Preacher thinks it is punishment for nearly making me crispy in a fire. But I know he won't.

I don't think Preacher is capable of thinking he's wrong, but it doesn't matter now. I need to let it go and get on with my adventure.

Then a vision hits me again. This time I am sent to my knees, overpowered by the sight of the tunnel. I am inside and there are giant moss-covered boulders blocking the path here and there. The voice is still a whisper but at a volume that makes my head ring. "Come."

I yell out, "I am coming, for the Light's sake. Let up on the vision, why don't you?" The watery world fades and leaves me folded up on the ground. Sam comes over and licks my face, then whines a bit.

"I'm okay, Sam. Just another stupid vision." I hope they don't get much worse. Whoever is doing this to me has to know it's painful, right? What if it isn't human? What if it's like Preacher says, and the all-powerful Light is doing this? I don't have any better explanation, but I do hope the Light isn't going to accidently kill me with these visions.

We come to a stream, the road connects to a stone bridge that arches over it. It's maybe three meters across. I take off my pack and decide to eat lunch.

I whistle for Sam, who comes running. I pull out his dish and pour water for him. But he just sniffs it and sits on his haunches. "Fine. Be picky then." Sam prefers stream water, I figure.

I pull out a loaf of bread and some smoked meat Ma gave me. There's cheese, but I'm going to save that. I have no idea how long it will be before I will see proper food when this is gone. I have my bow and a knife to hunt with, and Sam is good at rooting out gophers, but food prepared at home is going to be scarce sooner than later.

I sit and eat, tossing scraps to Sam while I look at the scene in front of me. It's grassy hills as far as I can see. I know there's a forest ahead, but I won't reach it until tomorrow evening if I don't dawdle.

I hear thunder. Looking behind me, I see the rain coming. It's going to drench us, I'm sure. I get my belongings and, holding my sandwich, I duck under the bridge to wait out the storm.

Sam follows me in and growls. I look around and see a rather large green thing with yellow eyes and hairy pointed ears watching me.

It says, "No humans allowed. Get out."

I don't know what to say. This thing is a troll. Like in the stories, only this isn't a story.

"You're a troll."

"You think I am something different? Maybe you think I am a butterfly?" The troll interlocks its hands and makes fluttering gestures. "Whatever, you will leave. This is my bridge."

"But it's wet out there."

It says, "What do I care? This is my bridge. Go find your own."

Sam growls, looking dangerous. It surprises me to see him get ill-tempered like this. I had no idea he could look so intimidating.

The troll says, "Don't let that dog near me. If it comes near, I'll, I'll ..." It looks around and picks up a stick. I think it looks more dangerous than it really is. I think it even looks a little scared, which is funny. I start laughing, holding my belly and chuckling.

The troll says, "Stop that! Chortnel is not a troll to laugh at, you puny human!" It waves the stick at me, which makes me laugh even more. I can't help it.

I say, "I'm sorry, you just caught me by surprise. You are Chortnel?"

Chortnel pulls its lips back, revealing sharp teeth. "Yes, puny human, I am Chortnel. Now that you tricked my name out of me, tell me yours."

"Tricked you? I didn't trick you. I'm Hawk. Hawk Archer, and this is my dog Samuel. I named him after my favorite bard."

"Sam Pettifog? I know him. He's a mean drunk."

I blink. "How does a troll under a bridge in the middle of nowhere know a famous bard like Samuel Pettifog?"

Chortnel shrugs. "I've lived a long time and not always here. I went to a Hadza so I could make offspring with another troll."

I say, "Offspring? You mean like a baby? What is a Hadza?"

Chortnel turns and says, "Like this."

On Chortnel's back, a small green face starts to appear. Little hands are emerging and below, two small feet. I'm not sure what to say.

"How? I mean... never mind, I don't want to know."

Chortnel turns back around. "A Hadza is a meeting for all trolls. We get together every once in awhile and do troll things until we can't stand each other anymore, and then we leave to be alone again."

I have to ask, maybe it's a human thing, "So, you are female then?"

"You may call me so if you need to."

Lightning strikes close, with a thunderclap right behind it. Samuel whines, and I put a hand on his head and give him the rest of the sandwich. The storm is right over us. I can feel the wind buffeting me from either end of the bridge. I try to reach out to the lightning, just to see if I can, but nothing happens. If I have some new power, it's only usable in times of stress, I guess.

A vision takes me then, this time so powerful I cry out. Chortnel's eyes grow wide. She says, "You are a vision seeker. What has given you this vision?"

The vision passes and I say, "Uh, vision seeker? I don't know what you mean, and I have no idea where they come from." Then I realize what Chortnel means—not that I seek visions, but that the vision gives me something to seek.

I say, "When the visions take me, I see a tunnel in the dome that is west from here, through the forests and then the sand dunes."

Chortnel sighs. "The hole in the world. Trolls know about it. We don't go there, but we know about it."

I say, "Do you know anyone who's been through it to the other side?"

Another bolt of lightning flashes, and this time I feel a twinge. The world doesn't slow down enough so I can grab power, but it's there, a small itch between my shoulder blades. The thunder rolls over Chortnel's reply. Samuel whines again and tries to crawl into my lap. I hold him as best I can and ask Chortnel, "What did you say? I didn't hear that."

Chortnel grumbles, "I said there are stories of people going into the tunnel, but none where they ever come back."

I say, "Tell me more about being a vision seeker."

Chortnel shrugs as another bolt flashes. This time, to my surprise, I grab it. Chortnel's mouth is open, her face frozen. I see drops of rain frozen in the air. I bend the lightning and send it out towards the west, along the path we are walking. Then the world returns to normal and thunder rolls, clapping hard and near. Sam whines and barks a little. I nuzzle his neck. "Shhh boy, it's okay, I'm here."

Chortnel says, "Your dog should have been a cat."

I frown. "Why do you say that?"

"He's scared like a cat."

I shake my head. "He doesn't like loud noises. His ears are sensitive."

Chortnel nods. "Like a troll's ears maybe. We hear much better than humans."

The rain stops. Through the clouds the light is bright again as the lightning and thunder move off to the west.

My stomach growls. I rummage in my pack and pull out some smoked beef. I tear a stick in half, then I give part to Sam and offer the other part to Chortnel.

She cringes. "I don't eat dead meat." She gets up and goes to the stream. She wades into it, looking over the surface, scanning her eyes for something. In a quick movement, she plunges a hand into the water and pulls out a fat trout. She tosses it to Samuel, who catches it and chews, growling happily. Chortnel turns and darts a hand again, then pulls out another trout, which she bites the head off of.

Sam growls his happy growl and chews the trout, leaving the beef jerky on the ground.

"Live food much better for you and for your dog," Chortnel says. She tears another piece of trout off with her teeth and chews.

I say, "I'm good with cooked food myself, but thanks for thinking of Sam."

Chortnel swallows. "I'm going with you."

I say, "Okay, but I am going through that tunnel. If what you say is true, I won't be coming back."

Chortnel turns so I can see her offspring again. "Baby trolls need their own place. I was going to journey anyway. Maybe there will be a nice place for her on the other side of the tunnel."

I stand up, brushing off crumbs. "It's fine with me. Sam and I like having company. But I'm leaving now."

Chortnel stands. She is twice as tall as I am. She says, "Then let's be on our way."

We travel through grasslands, the air smelling clean, freshly scrubbed. Off in the distance, a forest becomes visible. There is something wrong though. I am too far away to tell what it is.

Chortnel says, "Fire. The forest is burning."

Chapter Five

Encounter

We walk towards the smoke in the far distance. Chortnel says, "Since you are good at tricking me, I might as well tell you about trolls."

I say, "I've never tricked you."

Chortnel nods and waggles a finger at me. "That is your best trick. But be quiet. We trolls love to talk, but we don't much care for interruptions." I pinch my lips together with my fingers to show her they are sealed.

Chortnel says, "In the beginning, the World was made by ancients who had immense power and knowledge. No one knows why they made the World and the Light. Some say there was a cataclysm that not even the ancients could stop, so they built the Dome to protect all the races. I think they made the Dome just because they could. But that is my opinion, and few trolls share it." Chortnel stops and looks at me, maybe to see what I think. I keep my face blank and lips sealed. She turns her attention back to the road and continues.

"The ancients placed us all here—humans, trolls, fairies, gnomes of various sorts, and fire eaters or what some call demons. We have all lived under the clouds for so long that we have forgotten what is outside of it. We trolls live the longest, but even we can't count back to the start of it all." Chortnel scratches her shoulder where her baby is.

I say, "Does the baby make you itch?"

Chortnel nods. "It means she is close to being drawn out. Probably a few weeks more. But you tricked me again, Hawk. Getting me off track of my story." Chortnel wiggles a finger. "You are very wily and cunning. I will have to keep an eye on you."

I say, "I don't mean to be. I'm sorry, go on with your story."

Samuel brings me a stick and prances around me with it in his mouth. I grab it and send it sailing through the air far in front of us. Sam takes off in a joyous run.

"You teach your dog to be silly?"

I shrug. "It's just what dogs like to do. Run and chase things. It's their nature, I guess."

Chortnel watches as Sam grabs the stick and comes bounding back. She continues her story. "So, when we all were first placed here, we had all the power of the ancients, but because we did not need it, we quit using it, then we lost it."

I frown. "You mean like magic?"

"Yes, and visions. Like the visions you have." She turns and looks at me. "You will be honest now, Hawk. Do you have magic too?"

I evade. "Do visions and magic always go together?"

Her mouth pulls back, showing sharp, pointy, yellow-stained teeth. I think she is smiling, but it sends a shiver through me. She says, "No one really knows. There are stories. No one has seen an actual vision seeker. There are only stories, but I think you are one. Seekers are always said to have powers like the ancients. Do you have magic, Hawk?"

I don't answer right away, but then decide I might as well tell her. "I just found out that I can move fire and lightning. Make it go where I want, but only sometimes. Most of the time I can't make it do anything."

"You will learn, I think. Something is pulling you to the hole in the wall. Something is happening." Her eyes narrow. "Long ago when we first were brought here, we were given purpose. No one knows what the purpose is or was, and many no longer believe it ever existed. They say it's just us wanting to believe we are more important than we are."

"But you believe different."

"I think you are going to find out. This is why I want to go with you. It's more than adventure, it may be important to all the races. You may be important to everything under the Light."

I say, "I'm just a guy who likes to wander around. Nothing special about me. Heck, my own village tried to burn me as a sacrifice."

Chortnel gives me that troll grimace that I am convinced is meant to be a smile. "But you got away. How?"

"I ran. There was a storm, and, in the chaos, I ran out of the village."

She shakes her head. "You should not be untruthful. Not to me or to yourself."

"They were going to burn me, like I said. When they were about to toss me into the flames, there was a lightning bolt and then the whole world froze. Nothing moved except me and that lightning bolt. I could see the white metal fire of the bolt moving towards me. I just knew in that instant what to do. I split it and made it cut the ropes tying me. Then I ran into the night and the storm. I think they might have chased me down again and brought me back to finish the job, but I also saw something else when the world stopped and the lightning bolt was coming at me."

Chortnel waits for me to continue. I stop and sit down. I think about that moment, and it comes clearer to me now. The flaw in the covering above the clouds. I hadn't really thought about it until Chortnel's question. Now, I could remember there was a wrongness above the clouds, something that made the light disappear. I had felt it, and I just knew how to fix it.

Chortnel asks, "Are you having another vision, Hawk?"

I shake my head. "No not exactly. I'm remembering something I saw and fixed with the lightning bolt."

"What did you see, Hawk?"

I swallow. "I saw a brokenness, a disconnect in the covering above the clouds. There were connections there that bring the light and one was broken." I wonder what that could mean.

Chortnel says, "It frightens you. You don't like thinking of it as a thing, something that might break down."

"If that covering can break down, then our entire world can break. We could all die in the darkness."

Chortnel gets up from her squatting position. "You ready to go?"

I say, "What? No, I'm not ready. I just told you the entire world could end and kill everyone, wipe us all out, and you act like it's nothing."

Chortnel shrugs. "Do you know of anything, Hawk Archer, that lasts forever?"

I sigh. "I thought the world did."

"Well, you were wrong. Perhaps this vision you have is of the Light trying to fix itself."

I laugh. "If that's the case, it made a mistake. I'm no great hero."

Chortnel says, "It is the nature of heroes not to know what or who they are. They think themselves ordinary, only doing what needs to be done." She scratches her shoulder blade. The baby is a bit further out now.

Chortnel bends down when Sam approaches with his stick. She takes it and flings it about three times farther than I can. Sam barks and takes off in a joyous run. Chortnel says, "Come, hero Archer, we should get going. I'd like to be at the forest before we camp for the night."

We continue walking, mostly in silence. We come to a creek with another bridge. Chortnel checks, but no one is living beneath it. "There are not so many trolls as there used to be, Hawk. These bridges would not be empty a century ago when I was young. Our race is fading away." She doesn't say it like she is sad about that, I think. She is just relaying a fact, like telling of a flower that went to seed.

I can see the flames now. The forest is still far off, and it looks like the fire is moving northwards. There are huge patches of black charred woods, and the smoke moves towards the north. Sam growls, then looks at me and whines. I squint at the horizon where the burned forest is emerging. There is something there, moving towards us.

Chortnel says, "You see them?"

I reply, "I see something. A pack of wolves, maybe? They seem to be running towards us."

Sam whines again and acts nervous, sniffing the air in front of us.

Chortnel says, "Those aren't wolves."

The things are running at a fast clip, heading right for us. They sure look like wolves. I squat next to Sam and keep an arm around him. I could pull out my bow but killing is something I avoid unless hunting for meat.

There are five of the things running towards us. They look a lot bigger than normal wolves. Their shoulder muscles are huge. They are panting as they run towards us, but they don't look tired.

Chortnel doesn't seem concerned. I ask her, "What do you think they want?"

"I'm not sure, but maybe it's about the fire."

Before long, the five 'not wolves' surround us. Each is at least twice my size. They stop and look at us, panting. Sam growls, but I hold him close. I do not want him to go all hero on me and try to take on this pack.

One of the larger ones comes closer, sniffing the air and looking at me, then at Sam. Sam bares teeth at the thing, though it could probably cut him in half with one claw or bite from those impressive teeth. The wolf thing gets up on two legs growls and looks like it is going to lunge for me.

This is too much for Sam. He breaks my grasp and leaps at the wolf, fangs bared. The wolf swats Sam away. Sam yelps and tumbles on his back. I don't hesitate but leap at the wolf. I have no idea what I'm going to do. I mean, I doubt I could scratch its hide, let alone do any major damage, but Sam is more than just a dog to me.

I grab hold of the thing's neck and decide I'll go for an eye. I expect it to swat me away or chew me in half, but instead it picks me up in its teeth and tosses me to Chortnel, who catches me. Before she can set me down, the wolf things start to change. They shrink, and where fur had been, clothing appears. Their jaws recede into mouths with human lips, noses and eyes appearing.

I blink and feel Sam next to me, nuzzling my hand. I reach down and ruffle his neck, letting him know he did good no matter the outcome. I look back at our attacker, and there is a tall blond girl about my age with skin more the color of milk than the gold-brown color of mine and all the people I have ever known.

I say, "Werewolves are real too? Are we going to meet fairies and dwarves next?"

Chortnel says, "We might Hawk Archer. You don't know of the other races?"

I say, "Where I come from only humans are real, trolls, werewolves and other things are just stories we tell at night."

I'm looking at the girl who appeared. Her eyes are green with flecks of brown in them. She says something in a language I've never heard. Chortnel answers her.

"What did she say?" I ask Chortnel.

Chortnel says, "She wants you to know she sees the love you have for Sam and he for you, and she is confused why you would burn down her forest."

Chapter Six

The Wolf Pack

The plant fiber around my wrists and ankles is strong. I exert pressure on them by trying to force my wrists apart, but it doesn't seem to be doing much. I look over at Chortnel. She is calmly walking next to me. She doesn't seem to be exerting any effort to escape.

I whisper to her, "Why aren't you trying to get out of these ropes? You're way stronger than me. I'm sure you can break them."

Chortnel says, "Yes Hawk, I could." She strains her wrists against the fibers, and they stretch a little.

I say, "Well then, break them and let's get away from these things."

The werewolf pack surrounds us. They are all in human form.

Chortnel says, in her matter-of-fact way, "If I get us loose, what do we do then?"

We are following the bank of a large brook, heading north, upstream through the grasslands. Clouds have formed and it's sprinkling, but there is no energy to the storm. No lightning I can use. Even if there were, would I be able to control it enough to take out all five werewolves? Probably not. I'd either kill someone or make a fool of myself.

"Okay, good point. But we need to do something."

I sigh and look around for Sam. He's nowhere in sight. I get the attention of the closest of the werewolves.

"Hey, what did you do with Sam?"

He snarls at me. "He's following us, we just chased him away, that's all."

"Don't hurt my dog, he's harmless and he just wants to be near me."

The snarler comes towards me fast. I have just enough time to see the face framed in jet black hair. His eyes are the color of mine. He could be from Hovel. He's huge, towering over Chortnel even. He backhands me hard enough to send me to the ground.

The blond girl says quietly, "Don't tell Haver what to do. He doesn't like it much."

I squirm and struggle to get up from the ground. Trying to stand with your hands and feet bound is not an easy thing. I can hear Sam behind me growling, but he keeps his distance, smart dog that he is. He will choose his battles and now, at least, I know he's near.

I finally struggle to my feet and say, "I will be careful in the future. My name is Hawk, by the way, and now that I've met Haver, what is your name?"

The blond one says, "You can call me Leader."

"Do the rest of your pack call you that?"

She shrugs. "I am their leader, so that is what I am called. Save your breath for something besides questions."

But of course, I can't do that. I ask, "Where are you taking us?"

Leader says, "We are going to sell you to the dwarves. They will give us passage to a new forest. You will be slaves and work in their mines."

"Slaves? Mines? I won't..."

I can't finish the thought as a vision takes me. This time the world drowns under an invisible ocean. Everyone's movements slow. almost like when I saw lightning. This time there is a sharp ringing sound, sort of like Preacher banging his meeting anvil, only so loud it hurts my ears. I feel a wetness in my ears, then I collapse on the ground.

"Come." The voice is so huge that it feels like my skull is going to split wide open. I lay looking up at the Dome. I have to find a way out of this predicament or soon, maybe the next one, a vision is going to kill me.

I come out of the vision to Sam whining and licking my face until Haver growls and rushes him. Sam cowers and scurries out of his reach, away from our group.

I sit up and put my head in my hands. The ringing sound doesn't fade away this time, but abruptly stops; my head feels like it is still vibrating even though I can't hear it anymore.

Leader asks, "What's wrong with you?"

Chortnel replies for me, "He's a vision seeker. He has visions of a task he must accomplish. The visions grow stronger the longer he stays away from seeking it."

Leader looks at Chortnel sideways and says, "A vision seeker? So not only does he control the lightning, but he is called by the Light?"

Chortnel shrugs. "Some say that is true. Others think it is some form of illness of the head, like with people who see the world differently and are hard to talk with."

Leader shakes her head. "Legends and fairy tales. He's got some kind of head sickness." She looks at the others, obviously considering some decision. She finally says, "We'd better get moving. We will get him to the dwarves before his head kills him."

One of the pack that is near, another woman with black hair and coloring like me, grabs me and shoves me forward. "Get walking."

I say, "Sure cutey, what's your name?"

She snarls, "I'm Donla, second leader."

"Are all leaders women?"

She shoves me again. "You ask too many questions. It will get you hurt. Move now."

We continue walking. The rain drizzles, and though I rarely do so, I say a prayer to the Light to bring me a nice big storm complete with lightning and thunder. The clouds are gray, but not the dark angry kind that brings that kind of storm. The Light doesn't seem to listen very well.

I'm sure I can take all five before one of them gets me, but Chortnel is right. What do we do after that? I work my way close enough to her to whisper again.

"If we get a good storm, I'm going to bring the lightning. Do you think you can help me subdue these people?"

Chortnel says, "We trolls may look ill-tempered and powerful, but we are mostly observers. We don't take to action like other races. We prefer to watch and observe, record for history."

"Great, maybe you can just trip one or two of them."

"I think that if you try to subdue these people, you will have to kill them, Hawk Archer. Unless you think you can control the power enough just to knock them senseless."

"I think if I don't at least try, these visions will kill me. It's either me or them. Will you help me?"

Chortnel doesn't say anything for a few moments, then replies, "I will think about this, Hawk. It is not in my nature, but perhaps you are right. Maybe you are not friend, but you are close, I think. I would not like to see you die." She looks as though she is thinking of saying more, but she keeps quiet. I wonder what secrets she might have that she's not telling me.

We walk on until the light fades. The night begins to descend on us. Leader signals something to the others and then transforms to her wolf form. Donla and Haver pick me up and place me on Leader's back, tying me down like a bundle of sticks. When I am secured, another of the pack transforms to wolf. Donla and Haver perform the same task with Chortnel.

I ask, "What about Sam?"

Donla replies, "He's a dog, he can run." The rest transform, but before Donla changes, she smiles and says, "If he's lucky, your dog won't be able to keep up. If he's caught by the dwarves, they'll fatten him up and eat him." She grins and transforms; the wolf's toothy open muzzle makes choking sounds that I take a wild guess are sounds of a wolf laughing.

The drizzling rain continues. I begin trying to reach out to the power, thinking if I could just find some in the clouds somewhere, I'd be able to harness it and set us free.

If I am careful, maybe I can just stun the wolves without killing them. Then we could at least escape and formulate a plan to avoid recapture. Doing nothing is not in my nature, and now that I know what is in store both for Sam and for me, I am getting frantic. I could try to drive him away, but even if I were freed up enough to do that, Sam would just hang back and be confused. He wouldn't stop trying to follow me. I know this because if someone had captured him, I would stop at nothing to follow and free him.

As we travel through the night, the few attempts I make at conversation are met with stony silence. Chortnel is far enough away that I can't hear her or talk to her. Talking to the wolves is useless. They might growl, but they don't speak to me.

When the lights come back in faded morning form, I can see we are moving towards a mountain. Dark and purplish, it reaches up high overhead, maybe all the way to the apex of the Dome.

I call out, "Chortnel, can you hear me?"

She replies, "I hear you, Hawk. What is it you want?"

Her voice sounds weary. I suppose we both are. The back of a running werewolf is no place for napping. "What is that ahead of us?"

"That is the mountain of the Dwarf King."

My stomach drops and I feel lightheaded. I turn as best I can to look behind us, but Sam isn't there. I turn back around as the forward motion stops. I can hear a thrumming; a low pitched noise that is growing louder. I strain to move my head around towards where it is coming from and get a glimpse of huge numbers of shaggy beasts running across the plains.

Leader lifts her muzzle and howls. The rest of her pack follow suit, and they all take off running. The faster pace is not any easier on me. I suppose that they are going to hunt one of these things. My guess is that holding the wolf form takes a lot of energy. Otherwise, wouldn't they have just stayed in wolf form and run all day as well as into the night?

A nice, fat shaggy beast would be just the thing for five hungry werewolves, I think. I wonder if they'd have the courtesy to stop and cook some of it for me. I doubt it, and Chortnel won't mind the raw meat. I'm not hungry enough, yet, to make the idea of bloody shaggy beast parts seem like a good meal choice.

The beasts' pounding hooves grow louder. Leader howls again, and I can just make out over her shoulder a beast running slower than the rest of the herd. The pack surrounds the unlucky thing and begins nipping at its hind legs. It stumbles but gets back on its feet quickly. It runs for the herd again, but I can see enough to know it's hopeless. The rest of the furry things are moving at a gallop, getting further and further away.

The wolves leap on the beast, and Leader moves under its belly, tearing into it. The thing bellows as the rest of the pack attack the hind legs, tearing at them until the beast falls and lies on its side breathing hard, struggling to regain its feet.

Leader tears a piece of meat from the belly and blood spurts. Soon, the wolves feed, tearing into the flesh with all the gusto I use with a large plate of beef steak and potatoes. I look behind us again, and this time I see Sam tongue lolling, his head up watching us. No doubt he's hungry. I hope he takes the time to eat something once the wolves start running again. I'm thinking he's going to need his strength.

There's a small breeze blowing now. The air has cooled off. I look at the distant mountain. It seems to come directly out of the grasslands and shoot up towards the clouds. The top can't be all that far from them, I think. The grass is dotted here and there with bits of violet, crimson, and gold. I wonder if I could make tea from the flowers. The village herbalist would know, no doubt, but I don't have a clue how it's done. I only know I'm thirsty and hungry and a nice cup of tea and some seared beast strips would be welcome right now.

As each werewolf tears off pieces of the carcass, they lie on the grass and chew on their lunch. My stomach growls, I'm sure they can hear it. I try to ignore my hunger and thirst and it's not easy at first, then another vision takes me.

This time it shows me an opening in the mountain with several armored short people with long white beards. Each holds an ornate axe obviously made for battle. I wonder at this, but the vision departs and after I blink, I realize I'm on my back looking up at the gray sky.

Chapter Seven

Vision and Seizure

My stomach growls as I watch the wolves eat. I think about grabbing a hunk of bloody meat. It makes me nauseous just to think about it though. Donla changes to human form long enough to unfasten Chortnel and me, and then changes back to wolf form. I think being a wolf makes it easier for them to eat the raw stuff. I decide to try communicating.

"Hey, how about letting me make a cook fire so I can eat?"

Leader looks at me briefly, then tears strips of bloody red meat from the carcass. Chortnel munches on some organ she pulled out of the beast. There is blood dripping from her fingers and her chin. She looks at me and says something to Leader in a growl. Leader growls back and Chortnel walks over to me.

She says, "Go gather some dried dung for fuel, then light a fire, Hawk. I'll save you some meat to roast."

I say, "It will be easier if my hands are free." I hold them up to Chortnel. She looks around. The werewolves are all busy with their meals, so Chortnel breaks her ties and then reaches for mine. She puts a sharp fingernail under one end of the fibers and slices through them. I rub my wrists.

I say, "Thanks."

Chortnel nods and goes back to her own meal, not hiding the fact her hands are now free. I suppose the wolves will tie us back up once they are done eating, but I'll make the best of it for now.

I whistle for Sam, and he comes bounding to me. I hug him, and he licks my face. "Good boy, Sam," I say and take hold of his face fur so I can look him in the eyes. "You stay away from these things you hear? I don't want you getting hurt." I hug him again, then get up and begin searching.

There are piles of dung here and there from the herd, but most are too fresh. I continue searching and find a few piles of dried stuff, which I gather together and drop near Chortnel.

I concentrate on the dung, imagining it's Leader and I am stopping her from hurting Sam. That doesn't work. Then I imagine it's Preacher who is trying to hurt Sam. Still, no flames pop into existence. When I begin imagining Stigs Blaat hurting Sam, blue flames pop up from the pile. I kneel and blow on the small flames, coaxing them into something I can cook with.

Chortnel hands me a branch skewer with hunks of meat on the end. I cook the chunks, not being too careful, as I think I'd better get this meal in me before we take off again.

I hold the meat close to the flames and imagine them growing higher and stronger. They don't, and I have to blow them back into existence twice before the meat is seared enough for me to eat it.

It's raw in the middle and burnt on the outside when I take a bite, but it tastes good. Some salt would make it better, maybe some garlic. I have no idea where to get that savory herb, but the thought of it makes me wish I'd put some in my pack.

The meat is tender, and I don't have to chew it much. I'm about halfway through the meat Chortnel gave me when all but one of the wolves lie down, heads on paws, and close their eyes. The one in wolf form, I think it's Haver, moves over and sits near, watching me eat. He transforms into human, sitting cross legged as he watches me.

"You try to run, and I'll kill you," he says.

I say, "You won't get much of a price for me if I'm dead." I'm not sure if that came out well enough for him to hear it, as I say it over a mouthful of shaggy beast. He grimaces but doesn't respond.

When I'm finished, I whistle for Sam. He licks the meat juices off my fingers and face. I hug him again, burying my face in his fur. Then I begin telling him he needs to stay away from me. I tell him there are people who will kill him ahead of us.

I don't know if Sam knows what I tell him. I know that sometimes it seems like he does, and also that at times it seems he doesn't understand. I think maybe he just ignores what I tell him unless he thinks it's interesting. Either way, I hope for the best.

I end by telling him, "If something happens to me, you run back to the village. Mom will take care of you. I don't want you out here on your own." He pants and licks my face. That's when another vision takes me and this time when the voice says "Come" and the vision of the tunnel presents itself, the sensations are too much for me. I black out.

When I come to, Chortnel and all the werewolves, now in human form, are standing around me, looking down at my face. The two whose names I don't know pick me up and set me on my feet.

Leader says, "See, he's fine."

Chortnel says, "The visions are getting more powerful. If we don't take him to the hole in the wall, he's going to die. The dwarves are not going to grant you passage for a dead human and a lazy troll."

Leader is looking at me, distaste on her face. She looks like she wants me to disappear out of her life, no longer to be her concern. She says, "We'll go wolf form and get to the Hold before night sets. The sooner we get him over to the dwarves, the sooner he's not our problem anymore."

Donla asks, "What if they bring these two along with us when they guide us to a new forest?"

Leader shrugs. "I don't see why they would. The slaves are kept inside the tunnels working the mines. There's no reason to think they will drag useless baggage along the mountain passageways."

Most of the others turned wolf by then. Haver is tying Chortnel to the back of one of them. Donla and Leader grab me. My instinct is to struggle, but it is useless. I can't outrun them, and there is nothing but grasslands from here to as far as I could see. Running would be useless and time consuming. I will have to wait and hope a chance presents itself once we get to the home of these dwarves.

The rain stops, and the clouds are white now, the color they get when there is little chance of rain. We travel on into the evening when the lights begin to dim. I am unable to see Sam, but I know he's back there somewhere, staying close but out of the way of these strange people.

It's been dark for an hour when the mountain is close enough to swallow up the points of light in the night dome.

The pack stops, and they all howl in unison. All but the two who hold Chortnel and me change into human form. Donla and one I don't know free Chortnel and then come to my wolf to unstrap me.

There is a grating noise, like a milling stone grinding grain, only on the scale of a mountain. A beam of light appears in the mountain's flank. It's a sliver at first, but still well over four meters tall. The sliver turns into a rectangle, and then the rectangle is an opening large enough to reveal a large tunnel entrance. Standing with their arms crossed are a dozen stout, short people. They all have beards that fall to their bellies, and none of them is even half as tall as I am. Their arms are large, and chests are easily as wide as my own, possibly wider. They all have grim expressions on their faces.

One of them speaks. "What have you got for us, and what do you want?"

Leader steps forward. "We have two slaves, and in exchange, we wish passage to a new forest. Our old one is burned down."

The one who has spoken swings a large battle ax over his shoulder and lets it go. The ax must have slipped into a holster on his back, because it doesn't fall to the ground. He looks at me and then at Chortnel.

"I suppose this scrawny boy and lazy troll are your goods for trade?"

Leader says, "The boy is much stronger than he looks, and smart as well. The troll is strong and can carry much weight. She can be persuaded to work." Leader nods to Haver, who turns Chortnel around, exposing the baby. The baby's eyes blink and its arms protrude enough that they wave about.

"Besides, you get two for the price with this one, Gamul."

Gamul inspects the little troll with squinted eyes. "Troll babies are a burden. Running around, biting people. Not worth the trouble." He strokes his beard. "What do you think, Sarus? Should we take them?"

One of the other dwarves stepped forward and examines me. "I think he'll do well. Seems well proportioned and firm." He pokes my stomach.

I say, "Hey, watch it."

The dwarf grunts but says nothing to me.

Gamul asks him, "Do we take the deal, Wuruch?"

The dwarf standing next to Gamul shrugs and says, "He'll last a year, I think." Wuruch strokes his beard. "That plus the trolls is payment enough for me."

I only hear the part about lasting a year. "Now wait a damn minute," I say, "you can't just trade me into slavery like this. I'm a person. I've got a quest. If you try and make me a slave, I'll bring the lightning down on all of you."

Wuruch turns and frowns at me. "What are you talking about?"

Leader steps between us before I can answer. "He's got delusions, but he'll work hard for you." Leader kicks backwards and her aim is impeccable. The kick hits me square in the crotch, sending me to my knees and forcing an 'oof' out of my lungs.

Wuruch puts his hands on his hips. "What does he mean by bringing the lightning?"

Chortnel says, "The boy is a vision seeker and is called by the Light."

I hope this will stop the deal and maybe we can go free, but Gamul says something in a tongue I don't understand. Wuruch nods and reaches into a pouch at his side. He pulls out a round copper bracelet, only it's too large to fit my wrist. I get the idea of what it's for a bit too late as Wuruch slides it around my neck and I hear a click. I reach up and grab the thing, but it's locked in place.

Wuruch wags a finger and there's a twinge of pain that shoots up into my head, similar to what the vision does to me, but much milder.

Wuruch tells me, "Now you listen boy. That copper ring is magic. All I need to do is wiggle a finger and it will shoot pain right into your head." He wiggles a finger again, this time a bit more energetically.

This time not only is there more pain, but I feel something else. Some sort of power shoots down my arms into my fingers. It's weak, and it dissipates as soon as the head pain stops. I notice it, but I am busy dropping to my knees and grabbing my head when it happens.

Wuruch says, "You behave yourself and you won't have to be disciplined. You understand?"

I nod my head. Wuruch waggles his finger again, and pain shoots back up into my head, power running down my arms to my fingers.

He says, "I want to hear you say it. Do you understand?"

"Yes, I understand!" I nearly shout it. I'm frustrated, angry, and humiliated. I already want to strangle this short ugly thing causing me pain. I can't imagine my opinion changing any for the better.

Wuruch wraps another copper ring around Chortnel's neck, then we all set off into the entrance of the mountain. I look for Sam, but he's nowhere in sight. I decide to figure a way out of this as soon as I can. I have not bested Preacher, saved myself from being burned alive, and endured the visions just to die in a mine working for these evil creatures.

As we enter the wide stone causeway inside the mountain's entrance, I flex my fingers, hold onto the memory of power in them.

Chapter Eight

The Mine Slaves

The hole in the rock is jagged. Sharp pieces of stone stick out here and there as if placed by some sadistic sorcerer to snare my clothes.

I say, "I'm not going in there."

Wexley, one of the other slaves, scrambles into the opening. "Come on Hawk, it's not so bad. Just watch out for the sharp rocks." He carries a torch. The flame flickers, making the sharp tooth-like projections seem to dance. I grumble but follow him in.

Wuruch calls after us, "Be sure to leave the red stones alone. Any other color you find, bring out a sample."

Wexley calls back to him, "I know my job, Wuruch. Just remember you promised us double rations if we find four colors."

I've been here just a day now. The dwarves wasted no time in putting me to work with a crew of five. Two were large ogres with tusk-like teeth protruding from dark, swollen lips. They didn't say much, only grunted and gave me the eye if I got too close.

Grain is a woman, tall and lithe. She keeps her ears covered, but once I saw one of them slip out from her hair. It was pointed like the dwarf ears. She has large eyes, green flecked with gold, and doesn't talk much.

Wexley says, "Come on Hawk, keep up. If you fall behind, you're going to get snagged on a stone tooth."

I ask him, "How did you end up here, Wexley?"

It gets dark as Wexley thrusts the torch through a small opening. He puts his head in and looks around. "Careful with this one, Hawk, there's a tooth hanging down. Go in slow." As he moves through the opening, the darkness swallows me.

This is not encouraging, as Wexley is slightly smaller than I am. In the flickering light of the torch I can see he fills the space. I am going to have trouble. It's only a few seconds, I think, before the light shines back at me through the opening. I blink at the sudden change and shield my eyes.

Wexley says, "Come on then, I don't want to spend any more time than we have to finding gems."

As I squeeze myself through the gaps in the rock, Wexley tells me his story.

"I grew up on a berry farm outside the kingdom of Wyre. King Brinson loved our berries and so we prospered, as not only did the king buy them, but word got around so that others bought them as well."

Wexley pops through a hole, and light flickers in my eyes. I blink to get them used to it. From the other side, he continues. "One season, something got into the berries. They made people sick and so they all, even King Brinson, stopped buying them. My father did what he could, but it was only a few months before we were starving, all of us. He sold me to a trader in order to buy enough food to feed the rest of the family."

Wexley is quiet and matter of fact in delivering this information to me. I feel guilty at thinking Ma had been a terrible mother to me. I'm not sure what to say at first. "Do you think of going back to them?"

Wexley turns from his inspection to look at me through the opening. "Why would I do that? They couldn't care for us all, and I'm the one they got rid of." He shakes his head, then goes back to looking around.

"You need to get in here," he says. "There're gems everywhere. We're going to eat well for days, my friend."

I slip my head through the opening, followed by my left arm. When my left shoulder clears, I begin shimmying in. Then I get stuck. I wriggle, trying to move my body forward, but I'm not getting anywhere.

"Wexley, I need some help here."

Wexley turns and looks at me. "Damn it Hawk, you plug up that hole and the air in here is going to go stale real quick." He comes over, sets the torch down where it would stay lit, and grabbed me under the shoulders. He yanks while I squirm. After three tries, he sits down, breathing hard. I haven't budged.

My voice sounds weak when I say, "Maybe you can push me back." I'm trying hard not to panic.

Wexley takes a hold and tries to push me back out. I don't move. Then something grabs my foot and suddenly I'm rushing backwards out of the hole. There's a sharp pain in my left shoulder, hot and sharp. Now I panic. I flail at the walls as I move backwards. I try to grab onto any outcropping near me, but I keep moving.

I don't think about why I'm moving backwards. It's just the building panic in me I think that makes me flail around. Then I'm out and falling to the floor of the tunnel, with Wuruch looking grumpy as usual. I hold my left arm in my right hand. The pain is a dull throbbing ache now.

"Quit fooling around in there." He flicks his fingers and pain seizes my head. The pain makes me realize, though, that I haven't had a vision since we entered the mountain hold. The thought passes quick through my head as the pain moves from my head down my arms into my fingers. I point them at Wuruch, and he goes flying down the tunnel. The look on his face is worth the meals I'm going to miss because of this incident.

Wuruch's eyes are wide, his mouth forming an 'O' as he sails through the air, finally crashing into one of the ogres. I don't know their names, nor can I tell them apart. The ogre is pushed off balance and sits down on the floor of the tunnel, surprise raising its eyebrows and making its lips form a mimicry of Wuruch's 'O' shape. They sit there, the ogre looking like a parent cuddling a child, both with the same expressions on their faces. I can't help it. I laugh. It takes control of me as I hold my belly and tears stream down my face. I laugh so hard I have to gasp to get air into my lungs.

I try hard to keep it in, but the relief of being free from that hole, and now from the pain in my head overwhelms me. I control it for a second and then let go a chuckle. It's just a short bark of a laugh, and then I swallow the rest down and cover my mouth.

Wuruch pushes his way out of the ogre's grasp and stands glaring at me. "What in the Light was that?"

I shrug and try to look as meek and small as I can. "I don't know. You went flying."

Wuruch looks at the ogres and points at me. "Grab him and follow me." The ogres move in their ponderous loping steps towards me. I guess I've just had enough of this slave business. I am not cut out for being told what to do. I never have been.

I flex my fingers, feeling the power in them, and with my mind I push the energy from my hands into the oncoming giants. They are both thrown to the ground, landing only centimeters from Wuruch. The other slaves have moved back, wide eyed and looking on as though they've seen the Light itself come to take them into the clouds. My left shoulder aches. I hold it as best I can.

I don't have a plan. I just hope whatever pops into my head will work. "Don't come near me. I'm getting out of here now." That's when the pain is back in my head. I think, at first anyway, that a vision has finally found me. But hands grab me from behind and I see that they are dwarf hands. The pain builds, but then so does the power coursing down my arms. I fling back at whoever is holding me and turn to see two of the dwarves rolling down the tunnel. Two more are holding Wexley, who is writhing in their grasp. I think at first that he's trying to escape, but then see that Wuruch is sending pain through him. I turn to face Wuruch and raise my arm. I point at him, but he says, "I wouldn't do that. You hurt me, and I'll kill your friend before you can get to me." He flicks two fingers, and I hear Wexley scream.

I grit my teeth and put down my arm. Wuruch smiles and nods at me. "You aren't as stupid as most of your kind." He nods to the ogres and says, "Grab him and follow me. Bring the boy with us as well. We might need him."

I don't struggle as one ogre grabs me and the other picks up Wexley. He's slumped over, eyes closed, tongue hanging out of his mouth. I feel pity for him. He's a good kid, gentle and kind to everyone he meets. It just seems to be his lot to suffer for the people he gets close to.

Wuruch leads us all to a main tunnel. Grain is quiet but I notice she is looking at my shoulder, which still throbs with each step.

The ceiling is over four meters above us. The passage is wide enough that the ogres stand side by side, and there is still plenty of room for people to pass by. Which they do, giving us all the room they can as they stare and walk by us. The dwarves look at us curiously, while the other slaves look at us with pity.

I'm thinking about Wexley's collar. That's the key. If I can remove his collar, Wuruch can't hurt him, and maybe I can gain the upper hand. I walk close to Wexley and eye the copper ring. It has a latch on it with no hasp that I can see. There isn't an obvious way to unhinge the thing.

Maybe if I can direct just enough energy to that particular spot...

Wuruch calls to me, "Hey, what are doing?"

"I'm following you. You said to follow you, so that's what I'm doing." I realize by repeating myself I'm showing my nerves. I take a breath slowly, then exhale, letting my body relax a little.

Wuruch stops in the middle of the busy thoroughfare. High above, giant torches provide light to the entire causeway. Some of the light flickers on Wuruch's mug, making him look even meaner than I know him to be.

"I'm warning you, you try anything and this one," he nods towards Wexley, "is as good as dead."

I say, "You won't do that."

Wuruch says "No?" Then he walks to me and looks up into my eyes. He may be a lot shorter than I am, but he's still intimidating. "Why won't I, smart guy?"

"Because if you do, I'll kill you." I say this without emotion, but there is a cold fire in my belly. I can feel how good it would be to send power directly through Wuruch's head.

The ogres grunt, then one of them says, "We go." The one holding Wexley pushes him forward, making him stumble. The one holding me pushes me into Wuruch, making him the one who trips. He falls to the floor of the causeway.

When he gets up, he has a smile on his lips. It looks a bit ferocious. He lifts a finger to the ogre who pushed me, and it falls to the causeway floor, screaming in agony. Wuruch's eyes look hungry and excited.

He makes the ogre squirm for what seems an hour before lifting his finger and sneering at the giant, who is down on its hands and knees, breathing rapidly.

"Don't test me, ogre. I'm in a mood to destroy and it might as well be you if it can't be him." He gestures to me, then there is a surge of pain to my head. Wuruch, I think, did it without thinking. I channel the pain into energy flowing to my fingers and make a gesture myself behind my back. I hear a faint clinking sound from the direction of Wexley.

I really have to bite my lip hard to keep from gloating. The time isn't here yet for Wuruch to know what I've done, but it's coming. It's coming soon. I hold my left arm in my right hand and make every effort not to smile.

Chapter Nine

The Prisoners

Wuruch locks the door on us and grins at me through the bars. "I'll be back once the council decides what to do with you, Hawk Archer. In the meantime, you three behave yourselves." He gestures to the ogres, who fall into step behind him. I strain to reach the collar on the one who had been tortured. I wanted to see Wuruch's expression when he and the ogre realized the collar no longer worked. But it didn't work, or at least I didn't sense that the collar came loose. I couldn't see it, but I didn't feel any power leave my fingers.

Grain takes my left arm in her hands. "Let me see this."

Her hair is covering her ears now, and I am growing used to the strangeness in her eyes. She seems fragile but she grips my arm and holds it still. She's much stronger than she appears to be.

I hiss as she undoes my shirt and slowly pulls it off my left shoulder.

She looks at it and says, "You dislocated your shoulder. I'll have to push it back in. It will hurt a lot." She runs her fingers over the skin of my shoulder, and I feel a cooling sensation.

I said, "You have magic?"

She nods. "I'm an elf. We all have the magic of healing." She gently moves my arm around. I don't know what she's doing, but I don't want to think about it either. The deep, hard aching there is a little less intense now.

She says, "My magic should help a little to numb the pain. You are a human, aren't you?"

"Yes, Wexley here and I are human."

"Did you know each other before being a slave?"

I'm about to tell her no, when there's a sharp pain in my shoulder and a popping noise as she pushes on my arm hard.

I exclaim, "Ow! The light take you, that hurt!"

She looks at me wide eyed. "I told you it was going to. Why are you surprised?"

I don't have a good answer to that. She runs her fingers over my shoulder, and there is a coolness that sinks into it, right down to the bone. Soon my shoulder is numb and there's no pain.

She says, "Try not to move it for a few hours. The inflammation will go down soon."

She sits back against the wall and asks, "What's it like being human?"

I sit back as well and am thinking of something to say when Wexley speaks. "Well, we don't have magic." He looks at me. "At least most of us don't. We have to heal things naturally or let them die."

"Humans make things, like carts and swords. Things of metal and wood, right?"

Wexley and I nod assent. Wexley says, "Don't elves make things?"

She says, "We make clothing and homes to live in. We can work wood to do what we need. But we don't have the ways to work metal." She looks at us quietly for a few moments, then says, "Can humans fix what is wrong with the World?"

I blink. "What makes you think there's something wrong with the World?"

She looks at me, turning her head to the side a bit. "You haven't noticed anything strange happening? Lights not coming on in the day, rumbling noises behind the cloud walls?"

Wexley says, "There was a big wind not long before I was sold. It whipped itself into a living devil and tore up whatever was in its path. Is that the kind of thing you mean?"

Grain nods. "The World is coming apart. It needs repairs. I was sent from the Elder Council to find humans who might know how to make those repairs."

Wexley and I look at each other.

Wexley says, "I don't know of anyone like that. No one knows what's above those clouds. Whatever it is, we don't know how to fix it."

Grain looks at me. "You have magic. You are of the Light, I am told. Maybe you can fix it."

I recall what I'd done to make the light come back. It had been clear to me in that moment, but now the memory is fuzzy.

"I did make a repair, but I have no idea how I did it." I explain by telling them the story.

Grain says, "Maybe the Light chose you to mend things in the World. Maybe you will get better at it with more practice."

I say, "I have no idea, but first we have to get out of here." I lean forward and tell them my plan. I take Wexley's collar off him.

"When Wuruch returns," I continue, "I will have Wexley's collar hidden but touching me. Wexley, you will have to hide your neck so he can't see the collar isn't there, then you must pretend it hurts, okay? If Wuruch thinks he's not hurting you, he'll be warned."

Grain says, "He won't be alone. He'll have the ogres with him, and maybe some other dwarves."

I nod and say, "I hope he does. Once he sends pain to Wexley's collar, I'll have enough power to release their collars and yours, Grain. We'll let the ogres have Wuruch, then we'll be on our way out."

It feels like a sure-fire plan to me. Grain doesn't seem as convinced. I add, "We can do something and get out of here or wait around to die in the mines. It's your choice, Grain."

She shrugs. "I suppose we should at least try." She looks thoughtful as she stares into my eyes. I feel an itch back behind the eye sockets. I blink but the itch remains until she looks away. She says, "Getting away from them is one thing. Finding our way out is something very different."

I say, "I have a friend here, a troll who knows his way around, I think. He's very smart, anyway."

Grain says, "Trolls are usually kept in the library if they behave themselves. Otherwise, the dwarves use them like they do the ogres."

I feel a little excitement now. "Do you know how to get to the library?"

Grain nods and says, "It's not just knowing the way, Hawk. If dwarves see the three of us wandering around alone, especially if they notice we have no collars, they will be on us before we can move ten meters."

I ponder this. "I will make my collar obvious. You two will have to do what you can with your hair and your clothing to cover your necks. It's the best we can do."

Wexley asks, "What if a dwarf stops us and asks where we are going?"

I tap my lower lip with an index finger, a gesture I use to help me when I'm thinking. I decide maybe the truth will help us here. "We'll tell them we were sent to the library to get a troll named Chortnel."

Grain says, "If they don't believe us?"

"We'll see what we see when we see it." An expression my father was fond of, may he rest in the Light. I hear a noise and whisper to the others to be ready. But it's just a young girl bringing us food and water. She doesn't look at us.

I say, "Hello, I'm Hawk, and these are my friends Grain and Wexley. What's your name?"

She doesn't seem to have heard me. She keeps her head down as she slides the bowls through the slot near the ground and then three skins holding water. Without ever looking at us, she turns and walks out.

I watch her walk away and say, "This is an evil place. If I can, I will remove all the collars so there can be no slaves."

I pick up my bowl and look into it. There are chunks of some kind of meat swimming in porridge. I think of what the werewolves had said about the dwarves eating dogs, and my stomach is queasy. I put the bowl aside and drink from a skin. It's water, brackish and a little swampy tasting, but I'm thirsty.

The other two finish their bowls. Wexley is eyeing mine. I slide it over to him. "I'm not hungry. Go ahead."

Wexley grins and then looks at Grain. He offers the bowl to her, but she shakes her head. She sits cross legged against the wall and closes her eyes, hands on her knees, and I think she's sleeping but her breathing is regular and methodical. I sit back against the wall and think over what I need to do.

First, subdue Wuruch and release Grain and the ogres. Two, find the library and release Chortnel. Three, find the exit and get out of this underground prison. Four, find Sam. Five, get to the hole in the wall before the visions kill me.

I have no illusions that once I set a step outside the dwarves' mountain home, I will start having the vision again. I will just have to deal with it when it comes. I can't stay here, and if there's a way through the tunnels to the hole, I won't take it without Sam. Maybe Chortnel can carry me if I black out from the visions again.

I hear noises, then Wuruch appears with the two ogres. The first thing he does is waggle a finger at Wexley, who howls in pain and grabs his neck. Wuruch seems satisfied and unlocks the door to our cell.

Wuruch instructs the ogres, "Grab the humans, but leave the elf here."

I say, "Why don't you do your own dirty work, shorty?" I know it's weak, but I spit on him to add more insult. It lands on his cheek. He lifts a finger and Wexley screams while I grit my teeth. The pain is so huge, I think I'm going to pass out before I can channel it to my fingertips, but even though my vision gets dim and the pain sears through me, I channel power to the collars on the ogres. They clatter to the floor.

Wuruch stops his magic, then both he and the ogres spend a few moments staring at this impossibility. I take the moment to grab Grain's collar, then rush Wuruch. I place it around his neck and snap the catch into place.

Wuruch grows wide eyed and yells, "Take him! Get him now!" He waggles his fingers at the ogres, but nothing happens. They are frowning down at the collars on the floor. One of them grabs its neck and rubs where the collar should be.

Finally, it seems to penetrate their brains that Wuruch can no longer hurt them. I see one of them smile and reach out for Wuruch.

"No, don't you dare! You'll be killed if you touch me! The guards will be here before you can escape this room!"

They grab him, each holding one arm, then begin a tug of war. Pulling Wuruch back and forth, he screams in pain.

I think about what he said about the guards. I say, "Wait! Maybe we can use him." The ogres look at me while they continue tugging

Wuruch between them. I think they must be toying with him, as I doubt it would take all their strength to pull an arm off the dwarf if they wanted to.

"Look, we all go together. We'll use Wuruch to get us out of here."

The ogres stop playing with Wuruch and one of them speaks for the first time. "I am Sage, and this is my sister Dust. What is your plan?"

"It depends on Wuruch." I look at the dwarf. "Do you want to die here?" Wuruch shakes his head. "Then tell me how these collars work. How do you make them cause pain?"

Chapter Ten

Finding Chortnel

Wuruch sneers at me, "You think I will help you?"

I say, "Yes, I think you will if you don't want the ogres playing tug of war with you."

Wuruch smiles and crosses his arms. "I am not a traitor. You can have them pull my arms off, but I'm not going to tell you anything."

He looks so smug. I see him glance at the entrance. I don't consider what that means. I'm trying to come up with a plan. I need to get to Chortnel so she can help us get out of here and I can go find Sam.

I hear voices, but it's too late to do anything. We all stare at the entrance as four dwarf guards, in helmets and armor and carrying short pikes, enter. They don't notice us at first. In fact, they are deep in discussion about some sort of game.

"Phebly can shave Ose's beard at forty paces."

"Bah, Phebly couldn't hit the Palace gates if they were right in front of his nose."

They freeze when they see us, stunned for just a moment, then they raise their pikes at us. I flex my fingers, but there's no power in them. I start to panic.

"Uh," I start, "we're just on our way to the mines, don't 'mine' us." I grin and shoo the ogres towards the door, each holding on to one of Wuruch's arms.

The four guards poke their pikes into our chests. "You aren't going anywhere. Wuruch, what's going on here?"

Before Wuruch can reply, Sage and Dust each grab the guard poking them, lift them off their feet, and toss them into the cage. The other two guards look to Wuruch, maybe expecting him to use his magic on their collars. It would be what they had seen happen over and over again. It's unfortunate for them that their hesitation gives Sage and Dust time to toss them into the cage as well.

I say, "Take their pikes from them, and their armor. Do we have anything we can muffle them with?"

Grain says, "We can take strips of clothing."

"Yes, that's good, let's do that."

Grain takes a knife from Wuruch and gets busy ripping bits of cloth from the dwarves' clothes and stuffing some in their mouths, including Wuruch, then using more strips to tie around their heads and hold the gags in place.

I look at the armor and then at Wexley and Grain. "I'm not sure I can wear this stuff, but let's try. Each of you put on the armor, also put a set on Wuruch, and I'll try to squeeze into the last bit."

Wexley and Grain are just a little taller than the dwarves, so they put on the armor no problem. The ogres hold Wuruch while Grain and Wexley dress him in the armor. I try to put on the last set but I'm just too tall for it. The leggings only come up to mid-thigh, and they make it impossible for me to move.

"Okay, so you two are going to act like guards. Sage and Dust will march behind Wuruch. Make sure your shields are down over your faces."

Grain says, "Why don't we just leave Wuruch here with the other four? What's the sense in having to waste our energy on him?"

I say, "Because he may be helpful to us in getting out of here. Once I find Chortnel, we'll head for the entrance, and he will meet with minor accidents if he doesn't help." I look at Wuruch. "Nod your head if you understand what I'm telling you."

Wuruch nods his head. He makes a muffled noise, trying to say something, but I cut him off. "Save your breath, I don't want to hear your nonsense right now."

I have my collar plus the other four. I do the best I can to keep them close to my skin. I am not sure what might happen if all the collars are triggered at once. I'm either going to light up like a thunderstorm or have enough power to take on a whole army of these dwarves. Maybe both.

We move out. The ogres each have a hand on one of Wuruch's shoulders. Grain seems to have a little trouble with her pike.

I whisper to her, "Use both hands." She's leading the way as we enter the main street. I concentrate on looking subdued. I think it's working as we move on. Some people are giving us looks, but so far, I haven't seen any of the slave masters. There are a few non-dwarves that pass us, but they all look at the road and concentrate on what's in front of them, never looking up.

Grain turns left onto another street. This one is not quite as busy. At the end I see a large white domed building with round bulbs on top and spires sticking out of the bulbs. There's a staircase made of some white stone that is streaked and flecked with gold.

We climb the steps. It's a long ways up. We get halfway up the stairs when Grain sits and Wexley sits next to her. Dust and Sage grunt and sit as well.

I ask, "What are you doing?"

Grain says, "I have to rest." She's out of breath. Wexley looks the same. They are both sweating inside the armor. I look around us. No one seems to be paying attention, and the foot traffic is light on the stairs. Considering the effort it takes to mount them, I understand why.

"Okay, but we can't stay here like this. Someone will eventually notice."

Grain nods and regulates her breathing. She breathes in slow and deep, then lets it go in a slow rush. Wexley is sitting, the pike pointing up at the torches way over our heads. We are high enough that I can see there are rooms carved into the rock all around us. There doesn't seem to be an untouched surface anywhere in sight. There are stairs connecting all of it, and down at the bottom is the main street leading off in two directions with narrow cross streets.

When Grain and Wexley recover, we resume our climb. Wuruch is silent. Apparently, he's given up the idea of resisting us. He walks up the stairs with an ogre on either side of him. We are so high up now that when I look behind me it's a little scary. The street below is so far that if anyone slipped and tumbled out of control, say because of dwarf armor, they'd be beat to a pulp.

I edge a little closer behind Grain and Wexley, watching in case they slip. We are now about twenty steps from the top, or at least to some sort of plateau.

We arrive at the top of the stairs. There are a few more leading up to doors that stand open. They are massive and seem to be made of stone. Opening and closing them must take a lot of effort. We walk up and through the doors. The hallway is cool and quiet. A few dwarves move, some having hushed conversations. There are tables, huge and sturdy but low to the ground. Dwarves sit in chairs around them reading parchment scrolls or books.

There is a desk in front of us, carved from the white stone and flecked with gold. Behind the desk is a troll, and behind the troll are row after row of shelves packed with books.

The troll looks at Wuruch. "Can I help you?"

Wuruch doesn't say anything. I say, "We need to find a troll named Chortnel. She would have come in just a day or two ago. She has a baby." I point to my left shoulder, turning slightly to indicate where Chortnel's baby is located.

The troll nods. "Yes, she is in records. You want to speak with her?" She looks from me to Wuruch, not showing any surprise. I suppose that's a troll thing. Chortnel never seems to get flustered by anything.

"Yes, where can we find records?"

The troll points to a hallway. "Go down there past the fountain and the Igly statue. Take a left at Barsen's painting. Straight on from there, you'll see a sign on the office door."

"Thank you." I begin walking that way, and the rest of the group follows.

"Be careful. There are dwarves roaming about watching for you, Hawk Archer."

I freeze and look back at the troll. She has a blank expression. She says, "Go. Don't waste time staring at me. You may find me fascinating, I'm sure, but you need to keep moving or they will catch you."

I nod. "Thank you. Err, what is your name?"

The troll shakes a finger at me. "Chortnel warned me you are wily, Hawk Archer. You must go, and you may not trick my name from me."

I nod. "Right. We'll just go." I walk away. When we are out of earshot I ask, "Does anyone know what she was talking about in those directions she gave us?"

Grain says, "The Igly statue, then take a right at Barsen's painting. Then straight to the sign."

I say, "Great, you lead, Grain."

Grain leads past a fountain. We come to a statue of a dwarf. It's huge, standing five meters high. The figure is carved from the gold flecked stone that everything in the library seems to be made of. Igly is reading a book and holding one of the copper collars in his other hand. I idly wonder where the dwarf women are. Every one of them I've seen has a beard. They must keep them sequestered somewhere.

A little farther on, we come to a giant portrait showing a mountain and two armies lined up on a green field in front of it. On one side there are dwarves holding various instruments of war, and on the other are human looking soldiers, here and there a pointed ear poking out from under a mop of hair and a few green skinned trolls and ogres. We turn right.

Grain continues until there's an oaken door with round rings made of brass. She eases one open and peers in. Then she pulls on the brass ring and the door easily swings open. I step inside and feel a pike touching my neck.

"Hold right there. You move, you die."

"You said you would not kill him." The voice belongs to Chortnel. I don't dare turn my head to confirm though.

There's a hissing noise coming from the direction of the voice, then silence.

A voice says, "You will remain quiet, troll, or you get more pain." A dwarf strolls into my view, He's much older looking than the rest. A jeweled crown of gold sits on his head. The jewels are red, green, sea blue, yellow, and turquoise.

"So this is the human wizard?" He's addressing Wuruch. Wuruch answers with a muffled moaning sound.

"Someone take the gag from Wuruch."

A dwarf stops poking me long enough to go to Wuruch, pull off his helmet, and ungag him.

The crowned one asks, "What were you saying, Wuruch?"

"He has all the collars. The ogres can't be controlled."

Dust and Sage growl and pick up two of the guards that now surround us. They hurl the small warriors into the others and send a half dozen rolling across the floor. I turn and see there are six more guards who now have surprised looks on their faces. I have the distinct impression that these dwarves haven't been challenged by slaves ever, or at least in a very long time.

I use the diversion to slip a collar around crowned one's neck. I feel a stab of pain from the other collars, and I see a richly dressed dwarf waggling fingers at us. He doesn't seem to notice that the king, assuming the crown means he's a real king, is writhing on the floor. I feel power returning to me, so I zap the slave master and Wuruch for good measure. The guards back off a bit as Dust and Sage advance on them.

I see Chortnel now and pop her collar off. I say, "Did you tell these guys how to capture me?"

Chortnel looks sheepish and says, "I'm sorry Hawk, they tricked me."

Chapter Eleven

The King and I

I shake my head as Chortnel explains how she was tricked. I just don't understand how someone who knows so much can be so, well, dumb. I don't say this out loud of course, Chortnel being so proud, and I do need her to figure a way out of here. I have to admit she's become something of a friend as well.

I say, "Take us somewhere we can talk privately."

I look at Grain, Wexley, Sage, and Dust. "Can you guys hide these guards? Gag them and put them behind bookcases or something?"

Grain says, "We'll do our best." She begins ripping strips of cloth from one of the guards. Wexley helps her while Sage and Dust watch, frowning. I don't think they understand what to do, but I don't want to take the time to explain either.

I let Chortnel lead me away down a hall. I have a hold on the king, and I can reach out with my mind to the collar. It's hard to explain. I am not touching it with fingers or anything, I can just feel a part of me, some new place in me, reaching out to the collar around the king's neck. I touch it and the king jitters.

He says, "I hope you like pain, Hawk Archer. When I am done with you, you will be a whimpering puddle on the floor of my throne room. I promise you."

I say, "Right. Maybe I should get one of the ogres up here to stretch you out a bit. Would you like to be taller, king? What is your name?"

"I am Ruuc, King of the Fuutenhold, Ruler of all I see."

"Well, you're not the ruler of me."

Ruuc scoffs, "A temporary situation."

Chortnel opens a door and ushers us inside. There are torches around the room keeping it from darkness. The floor is made of rough cobblestones, and there is a sturdy table, low to the ground as all things are in this kingdom, held together by brass plates attached to the four corners.

Around the table are chairs made, or possibly carved, of the same wood. I don't bother sitting. "Chortnel, do you know how to find the way out of here?"

Chortnel nods. "There are two ways we can go, assuming you wish to resume your vision seek."

I say, "I do, after I get Sam."

Chortnel scratches her shoulder. I see that her baby is not yet out—"born" I guess would be the right word.

Chortnel says, "If you go out the way we were brought here, you could die from the vision."

The king interjects, "What vision? What are you talking about?"

Chortnel says, "Hawk Archer is a vision seeker. He is of the Light. The vision he has was growing very strong when the werewolves handed us over to your people. They have stopped since we were taken underground, have they not, Hawk?"

"I haven't had one since we were brought here no."

Chortnel says, "The mountain hold provides protection from the Light. If you leave, I am pretty sure you will have them again."

I sigh. "Only this time a vision could kill me."

Chortnel nods. I say, "I can't leave Sam. I have to go find him. Is there something we can do to keep the visions from happening, or at least from killing me?"

Chortnel thinks, pulling on her lip while she does.

In the silence, Ruuc asks, "Who is this Sam?"

I tell him, "Just a friend. He's outside the mountain waiting for us."

Ruuc won't let it go. "Why isn't he in here with the rest of you?"

I say, "He ran away just before your guards came out. The werewolves didn't have time to go after him." This is all sort of true and I keep looking over at Chortnel to see if she's going to be "tricked" into giving more information, but she's still pondering my question.

Ruuc settles back and says, "If you are a vision seeker, I will not keep you. There is no need for this." He fingers the collar I placed around his neck.

I am suspicious. "Why would you say that?"

The king's expression doesn't change; he looks serious. "If you are of the Light, only fools would make themselves your enemy."

I think about this. Chortnel says, "I'm sorry, Hawk I just don't know of a good way. Maybe if we put one of the guard helmets on your head, but I can't be sure that will work."

Ruuc speaks up. "I can help you. We can make you a metal suit that will protect you from the Light and its effect on you."

I look at Chortnel. "What do you think?"

Chortnel scratches her shoulder. "Dwarves are normally truthful. But I have known a few to be deceptive." Her weird yellow eyes get unfocused for a moment. "We can keep the King collared, but can you cause him pain?"

I nod. "I'm learning how to activate the things, yes."

"If we hold him hostage, we still need some sort of protection for you on the outside, plus one of his wizards could unlock the collar. If we release the king and he keeps his word, you will have that protection, but I think there might be a third option." She strolls to a wall where an elaborate tapestry is hung. "Look here." She goes to the tapestry and points.

I see gold markings on a deep forest green background. It looks like a map of some kind. Preacher had a few maps. I'd seen one when I was a kid and unrolled one of the scrolls on a visit to his house with Ma. This map shows four circles with some sort of mound drawn in the middle of each.

Chortnel points to the circle in the upper left. "The World is divided into four places, we call them quadrants. We are in this quadrant, here inside the connection hub." She then points to the mound in the center of the circle. "The connection hubs are places that connect all four quadrants."

I ask, "Then what is the cave I saw? That's where the vision tells me to go."

The king says, "There is a connecting cave that leads to the lower left dome. It hasn't been used in a very long time. By your reckoning, Hawk Archer, your year counter would have been about 70,000 the last time that tunnel was used."

I can feel an itch behind my eyeballs. So much new information. My brain is struggling, trying to sift through it all.

I say, "So there are four worlds?"

Chortnel nods. "There may be more, but troll stories always talk about four."

I am not going to ask her why she thinks there are more. It could lead to my brain leaking out through my eyes and nose again. I say,

"Okay, so four worlds that are all connected by these mountains and passages."

King Ruuc says, "Yes, we can travel to this quadrant, and this one." He points at the dome in the lower left corner and then the one in the upper right corner. "Each mountain has one of my relatives overseeing it. The tunnel you found leads to the lower left quadrant world."

I scratch my head, but the itch is inside it. "So who made all this? Is this the entire world? Is there anything else?" I look over at Chortnel. "You said there may be more. Why?"

Chortnel points a finger at the center of the map. "Here is the unknown. There are no tunnels or other ways to get to the center that anyone has found, but there are legends that there is something here. It's a large empty unknown space. Many think that is where the Light dwells, eternally manifesting the worlds we live in."

I look at Ruuc. "Have the dwarves tried to make tunnels there?"

The king nods. "We have, and there is a magic once you go too far in that prevents any further digging."

I ask, "What sort of magic?"

The king frowns. "No one knows, but if we try to dig into the rock in that direction, we reach a point where the rock can't be disturbed. All our tools and magic are useless on it."

Now is not a good time to think about what is in that area. I need to find Sam, then get to that access tunnel or use the dwarf tunnels to get there.

I say, "Let's take the king with us to the entrance." I look at Ruuc. "Once we are on our way out, I will release you."

I hear a click, then both the king and I look down as the collar that was around his neck falls to the ground. I look up to see all my companions once again are collared. Wuruch stands behind them, hands on hips and a large grin on his face. The other magician stands next to him. They waggle fingers, and all my friends drop to the ground writhing in pain.

But now I can remedy this situation. Whatever sense has been given to me about this magic stuff is getting easier to use. I smile at Wuruch. "I see you didn't bother with the guards."

Wuruch says, "We don't need guards. We have our magic."

I waggle my own fingers and all the collars drop from my new friends. They lie, gasping for breath and hold their necks. The ogres get to their feet, grumbling to each other. Drool drips from the corners of their mouths where their tusks curl out.

Wuruch and the other magician turn and run. Sage and Dust start to pursue, but the king speaks up.

"STOP! Enough of this. Wuruch, Oldit, come back." He turns to me. "Hawk Archer, I am free of the collar now, so believe me when I tell you, I am not going to harm you or your friends. We will do what we can to help you on your journey."

I have nothing to say at first, but I have to know. "Why would you help me? You made us all slaves, and now you're going to give me your help?"

The king looks at me while stroking his beard. He takes a moment or two before answering. "Hawk, you have visions from the Light itself." He looks at Chortnel. "Trolls wouldn't lie about such a thing." He looks back at me and says, "I think that power is growing inside you and if I try to keep you, that power is going to only get stronger, maybe strong enough to destroy my kingdom."

More guards show up is in a rush. The king raises his hand to halt them. Then he takes a step towards me.

"Now, I could just have you killed and believe me, that was a strong possibility at first. You put a damn collar on me!" The last is said just shy of being a shout. I can see the control on the king's face as he struggles to tamp down the anger and, possibly, humiliation. I guess I am destined to piss off those who have power. At least since the time keepers announced 100,000 years and this vision thing all started.

The king closes his eyes and takes a breath. When he opens them, he says, "I have been given reports for a few years now of things breaking down on the outside. The light not showing up, strange weather events, shaking ground. My scholars tell me there is something wrong with our world. You asked about digging into the center between the domes, Hawk. We would never have done that before the break downs. We never had a need to. We knew of the magic that makes it impenetrable and so we never tried, but now…" He grimaces, then continues. "Now, things are breaking down on the outside." He puts his hands behind his back.

The king seems to love the sound of his own voice, but I don't want to interrupt him yet. I think I know where this is going, and if it leads to me getting on with finding Sam and getting to that cave, I'm going to let him talk.

The king continues, "I didn't think much of it at first. The outside can crumble, we'll still be safe in this mountain. At least, that's what I thought, what my scholars thought. But in the last year or so, they have changed their minds." He comes a little closer to me and says, "If the outside breaks too much, it will affect us even in here. It could kill every living thing in the four worlds if it goes far enough, and there is no telling just how far the break downs will go."

I nod, beginning to understand. "So, you think maybe I can save the world."

The king looks me up and down, grimaces, and then says, "The Light take me, but yes. You, a boy, a human boy at that, just might be the answer to saving us all."

Chapter Twelve

Finding Sam

King Ruuc says, "Let's get you to the tailors so they can take measurements. I'm sure we can have a suit constructed for you within a week or so."

I shake my head. "I can't wait that long. Just take us to the entrance and I'll go find Sam."

Chortnel protests, "Hawk, that is not advisable. You could die the next time a vision hits you. I'll go out and look for Sam. He'll come to me."

Ruuc stops and looks us both over. "Who is this Sam?"

Chortnel replies, "Samuel Pettifog is Hawk's dog."

Ruuc says to me, "You are worried I'll eat your dog."

I clear my throat, silently cursing Chortnel and all trolls. "Well, the werewolves told me that dwarves eat dogs."

Ruuc nods with a serious look on his face. Then he grins and laughs heartily; the rest of the dwarves all laugh as well.

I say, "What are you laughing about? Eating my dog is not something I find very funny."

Ruuc says, "It's a legend, a rumor. It's not true. In fact, we dwarves don't eat anything but vegetables. We don't care for the taste of animals of any kind."

He motions his entourage to continue walking.

I ask, "So why did the werewolves say that?"

Ruuc says, "We let the rumors spread. It makes us look more fierce, more respected."

We are walking down a major street now. Dwarves are watching us, bowing to the king, and slaves are still moving with their heads down, watching their feet. High above, there are cliffs with buildings carved into them. I want to reach out every time a slave passes to touch their collar. I think I could release them all if I tried hard enough.

I think I might do that. It feels wrong, keeping people as slaves, making them do what the dwarves want. I'm not sure I can just leave this place without at least trying to do something for them.

I say, "Where I come from, there are no slaves. We all work to get things done, and we help each other along the way."

The king says, "There are many who disagree with our way of life." He looks up at the cliffs and points. "Do you see all that work up there? All those buildings and carvings? Without slaves, they would not exist. Without our slaves, we would not be able to supply the world with metals." He pauses again, then changes the subject. "If you want to find your dog, then go with Wuruch. He will take you to the entrance. If you survive, Hawk Archer, and I hope you do, he will bring you to me."

I reply, "No collars, and my friends all come with me."

The king shrugs. "This is fine with me." He nods to Wuruch and leaves with his guards.

Wuruch looks at me. "You think you will avoid the collar, Hawk?"

I smile at him. "Do you?"

Wuruch laughs. "If you were a dwarf, I think I might grow to like you. Come on, follow me. I'll take you to the entrance."

We all fall in with Wuruch. Sage and Dust flank us. Wexley and Grain follow behind me and Wuruch.

Chortnel and I keep pace with Wuruch and make conversation. "Have you dwarves always kept slaves?" I ask.

Wuruch eyes me. "Since one of our smiths, Siisley, invented the collar. That was a long time ago."

Chortnel adds, "One hundred and forty-eight years."

Wuruch nods. "That sounds about right. Prior to, we mined tunnels and caves by ourselves." He looks around at the city. "This did not exist. We lived in a much different world."

Chortnel says, "Hawk, are you thinking you will free all of them?"

Wuruch stops and looks at me. "You do not want to do that, Hawk Archer. That would make you the enemy. Do you understand?"

I say, "I understand your king knows that my vision and my quest are very important." I decide to say no more and start walking the way Wuruch is leading us, Chortnel and the rest walking with me. Wuruch catches up to me and starts to say something, but I cut him off. "You treated me and my friends like we were less than animals. Your warnings and threats mean very little to me, Wuruch. You may have magic, but I have power."

I'm not sure I really do have the power to stop him if he decides to do something about me, but none of the dwarf mages have shown an ability to make magic other than on the collars. I think they must need the metal to channel their energy.

Wuruch doesn't say anything more about slaves or threats. He leads us to a large black iron gate. In front of the gate stand four ogres, all collared of course.

Wuruch tells them to open the gates and they comply. We pass through and continue on into a tunnel. There are no cliffs here, or buildings, just a smooth tunnel about five meters tall and maybe eight meters wide. I can see light coming in from the end of the tunnel. The great doors that had been closed when we arrived must be standing open.

Chortnel says to me, "Stay here. I will go and find Sam."

I say, "He may not come to you. I should go and call him."

Chortnel says, "Give me a chance first. If I can't find him, or he shies away from me, I will come back to get you."

I think this is probably a good idea. I don't really want the pain unless I have to bear it to find Sam. I turn to the others and say, "So here is your chance to get away. If any of you wants to leave to go home, now is your chance."

Sage and Dust each put a giant hand on one of my shoulders. They utter something in their language, which I don't understand. Then Sage speaks, "You are friend, Hawk Archer. The ogres will not forget this. If you need our help, you only have to remember this phrase: *A'ach nabeknae g'la*. Any ogre will know you are our friend and give you aid."

I hug each of the big green people. "I'm going to miss you both. I wish you well and long life." Sage and Dust leave after hugging Wexley and Grain. I look to Wexley next. "You are free to go too. I hope you can find happiness somewhere, my friend." I take his hand, but he shakes his head.

"I got nowhere to go, Hawk. Besides, I think being around you is going to be an adventure, and who knows, maybe one day the trolls will tell stories of us." He smiles.

I hug him as well. I haven't known any of these people very long, but I guess when you go through the kind of stuff we went through together, you get close to people. I let Wexley go and look at Grain.

"Will you be leaving to go back to your people?"

Grain shakes her head, then blinks her cat-like eyes. "I took a mission to find humans that could fix what is wrong with the world. I think that you are that human, Hawk. So, until you fix what's wrong with our world, I will stay with you and help in whatever way I can."

I'm glad to have them with me. Wexley, because he is probably the first real friend I have had that at least sort of understands me, and Grain for the same reason, plus she could be very useful to us all.

I turn to Chortnel. "Okay, go find Sam and bring him here."

Chortnel leaves. I sit against a wall and look at Wuruch. "How do we get to the next quadrant?"

Wuruch says, "There are water tunnels leading to one of the quadrants, and to the other there is a tunnel much like this one, and the last one I suppose can be accessed from either of the other two, though I have never seen it."

I say, "Do you know of the hole in the world in this quadrant? The cave that leads into the wall itself?"

Wuruch says, "Yes, it was once a path for trains."

"What are trains?"

Wuruch clears his throat and continues. "Long ago, there were a lot of machines that did all sorts of things. Your troll can probably tell you more than I, but one of these machines traveled on steel rails. It had wheels made of metal, and it moved with the use of some sort of trapped lightning."

I remembered the rusted-out metal rails I had seen. "What happened to them? To the trains?"

Wuruch shrugs. "I suppose that people forgot how to fix them or how to make new ones. When one broke, it wasn't repaired, and no new ones were made to take its place. Eventually, the trains were forgotten. You can see the rails in some of the connecting tunnels between the quadrants. No one has seen a real train though, at least not that I'm aware of."

I asked, "What did they look like?"

Wuruch says, "The stories say they looked like giant metal caterpillars. You know what a caterpillar is?"

I nod.

"The trains were multi-colored and shined. They moved faster than the eye could follow when they got up to speed. There are renderings in the library of them. No one knows if they are accurately drawn, though. No one has seen a real train for a hundred lifetimes at least."

Grain speaks up. "There are tracks in a few places in the elven forests. They are mostly overgrown, but we also have stories of these trains. They are similar to what you say, Wuruch. Long and gleaming, faster than the fastest forest cat. Some say faster than the Light itself."

I think about machines that use lightning for power. There was some sort of lightning power in the wall above the clouds when I fixed it. The image is very fuzzy, but I got the idea the power ran through rope-like things to whatever made the light work.

Just then, Chortnel appears. She looks sad as she scratches her shoulder. "I could not find Sam, Hawk. I tried, I called for him, but I see no sign of a dog anywhere."

I stand up. "He's hiding somewhere waiting for me. I'll have to go and call him."

Chortnel nods. "I will go with you and bring you back inside if a vision takes you."

Grain stands as well. "We'll all go."

Wuruch sighs. "I might as well go. It's better than sitting here waiting on you all."

We walk out the entrance. I look up and see the sky is day bright. There is no telling what time it might be, but it's definitely daytime. I call out, "Sam! Come on Sam!" I whistle and then wait to hear his bark. There's nothing. I walk away from the entrance, and Chortnel follows me.

After ten meters, I stop and call again for my best friend. I wait and listen, but there is no answering bark. Now I'm worried. What could have become of Sam? Maybe he decided to head back to the village after all. This is the least worrisome possibility I can come up with.

I walk another ten meters and stop. I repeat the call and wait. There is a faint sound far off in the distance. I hear it again, this time a little stronger. I call again, 'Sam! Over here, Sam!"

Now the bark is unmistakable. It's Sam, and I'm relieved. Then a gong goes off in my head and the whisper is deafening. "Come." I feel the wetness in my ears, nose, eyes, and mouth just before everything goes black.

Chapter Thirteen

Emancipation

I open my eyes, but as soon as I try to sit up, I am made aware of what an anvil feels like when a smithy strikes it with a hammer. I put my hands to my eyes and give a yelp. It sounds weak, and I'm surprised the sound came out of me.

Rather than make a further attempt at movement, I just lie back, hands over my eyes, and groan.

I hear Grain say, "You've had a bad time of it, Hawk, just lie still for now."

I feel her put her hands on either side of my head at the temples. There is a coolness that seeps into my throbbing nightmare of a head, slightly dulling the pain.

"Can you tell me your name?"

"Puddin' tame, ask me again, I'll tell you the same." I don't know why I say that. Probably the feeling that my head wants to explode is making me a tad cranky.

"Ahh. Do you know where you are, Puddin'?"

I sigh. I'd probably find this conversation funny in my normal self with a normal brain. "Yes, and my name is Hawk Archer. I was just annoyed."

"I see." I can tell by the inflection in her voice that she is humoring me. "You seem to be okay. I must insist you do not go outside the dwarf kingdom again, though. I had to expend quite a bit of magic to keep you from becoming a drooling piece of meat."

The hands at my temple continue their healing. I can feel the throbbing diminish little by little. I'm suddenly very tired. I ask, "Is Sam okay? Is he here?"

Grain says, "He's well. He's with Chortnel and Wexley."

There is something odd in the way she says this, but I can't put my finger on it. The world is getting fuzzy and starting to fade away again. I sink back into unconsciousness.

When I wake the next time, there are no hands on my head, but the throbbing is gone. I sit up and look around me. I'm lying on a bed, a small table next to me. The bed is barely a half meter off the ground because it's a dwarf bed, I guess.

I sit up. My brain seems to be back to normal. No headache. It's then I hear a whine and look over just in time to see Sam as he jumps into my lap. I catch him, laughing, and hug him to me. He struggles out of my hug and starts licking my face. His backside moves quick as he swings his tail back and forth.

"I'm glad to see you Sam. I missed you a bunch." I laugh more as he finishes licking my face and lets me hold him close. I bury my face in his fur.

I hear King Ruuc say, "We almost lost you, Hawk Archer. That would have been a pity."

I look over and see Ruuc is standing with Wuruch. There are dwarf guards with them.

I ask, "Where are my friends?"

Ruuc nods to a guard, who drags over a chair next to me. The king sits and looks at me for a moment. "Your friends are safe. I'm keeping them in another part of the castle for now while we talk."

I look from the king's face to Wuruch. "What is it you want?"

The king laughs. "You are a smart one, Hawk. So very smart." He sighs. "I want to help you, partly because I think you are meant to do something historic, momentous, and world changing." He pauses and leans forward. "But also, because I want you out of my kingdom before you cause me a lot of headache and damage."

"I don't want to cause you any headache, Ruuc. I have my dog back, and all I want now is to get out of this mountain and on with my journey."

The king and Wuruch smile at me. "I wish I could believe that, Hawk. I really do. I want to trust you, but you see, we dwarves, well, let's just say we don't make friends easily with other kinds of people. We have good reason not to, but I'm not going to get into that.

He sits back in his chair now and stares at me for a few moments. He touches his fingers together one at a time in a rhythm. He doesn't seem to be aware that he's doing this. I'm wondering how he is going to make me leave his slaves alone. I've pretty much made up my mind I'm going to set them all free. I'm not sure I can reach out that far and wide, but I will reach as many as I can, and as soon as I get the chance.

But instead I say, "I really just want to find out why I'm being called. Just let me and my friends go. Show us the way to this connecting tunnel, and we'll be gone from your kingdom."

Ruuc nods. "I believe you, Hawk. I think you and I have come to respect one another if we haven't exactly become friends. But I don't get to make all the rules all the time. There is a council that expects me to answer to them." He shrugs. "They are a nuisance, but it works for us. I am careful not to upset them too much, and they are careful not to demand too much from me in return."

He leans forward again. "So here is what we are proposing. You and your dog will be taken to the underground lake that leads to the next quadrant. Wuruch will guide you to the other end of the tunnel, and when he returns, we will put your friends on another boat and send them to you."

I ask, "How can I trust that you will keep your word?"

Ruuc says, "You could always come back to rescue them if I don't, right?"

I'm not sure that is an option if I need to be guided across this lake, but I don't see many other options presenting themselves. I decide to bargain.

"Let Grain and Wexley come with me, and you can keep Chortnel with you until Wuruch returns."

The king thinks about this. He looks at Wuruch. "What do you think? Would our friend Hawk abandon this troll and try to set our slaves free?"

Wuruch says, "They seem to be good friends."

Ruuc strokes his beard. "Agreed." He sticks out his hand to me. I take it. Sam sits patiently by my side. He seems unconcerned by the dwarves. I am glad other species don't make him nervous.

The king nods to a guard, who goes off down an access way. The king says, "Follow me. I'll take you to the launch."

We walk a short way and turn down a lane that is deserted. I suppose there isn't much traffic going to the other quadrants. I ask, "Are the other quadrants part of your kingdom as well?"

Ruuc shakes his head. "No, there was a time when we dwarves went to war over that issue, but at least for now, there is a truce between us and the other two kingdoms we border. There has been no war for over a century now."

"Do the other kingdoms also keep slaves?"

"They do, and I would advise that you will need all of our cooperation to travel between the quadrants. I am not charging you because I happen to believe your quest is vital to everyone under the domes, but I can't say that will be true of the other kingdoms. They may not agree to give you passage, and trying to free their slaves will not help your cause."

I think about this. It is a problem. I don't feel like I can ignore all those people wearing the collars, being forced to live lives not of their choosing, but I do need to continue this quest. I will have to delay any action I decide. After this is all over, and if I still have the power over fire and lightning, I will form a plan to stop the practice.

The king says, "I will give you a letter of recommendation and gifts for the other rulers. The one who you will meet in the next quadrant is Evonne. She has ruled nearly as long as I have, and I think she will support your cause once she reads my letter."

I say, "Okay, I agree to leave your slaves alone, just bring me Wexley and Grain. You will put Chortnel on a boat as soon as Wuruch returns from his trip."

The king leaves with Wuruch. I call out, "Please bring us some food for Sam. I'm sure he hasn't eaten well in a while." Ruuc grunts his assent as they leave.

I sit on the ground and look Sam over. "Well now, you do look a little thin, good boy." I stroke his fur from neck to hind quarter. "I missed you." Sam licks my face and whines a little. The familiarity of our friendship makes me feel a lot better.

I will be even better once we are away from this place. I can almost see myself trusting Ruuc, but Wuruch is a different matter. I think he'd just as soon kill me as look at me.

There's a large boat tied to the dock here. Sam and I walk over and inspect it. It's big enough to hold a dozen people. There are three oars stowed neatly on each side of the boat. Each oar is attached to the sides by u-shaped wooden swivels allowing the oars to move forward and back, up and down.

I kneel on the dock and touch the water. Sam sniffs at it, but standing on the dock, he can't get very close. I have to reach down as far as my arm will go to touch my fingers to the water. It smells fresh to me.

Sam gets bored and runs to the beach, lapping at the water then sniffing the shoreline. After a while, I see seven dwarves coming and Wexley walking beside them. When they get close, he gives me a hug. "Hi Hawk, it's good to see you."

I say, 'Likewise, Wexley. Where's Grain?"

"Grain wanted to wait behind. She's helping Chortnel with some kind of research they think will help us on our quest."

I look at the dwarves, Wuruch is not with them. "Where is Wuruch?"

One of the dwarves says, "He's busy with some other project. We'll take you over and then come back for your friends. Get in the boat and let's get going."

This isn't the plan, but I can trust Wexley when he says Grain wants to stay behind. I'm not so sure about Wuruch. "What is Wuruch doing that is so important he can't come see his good friend off?"

The one who spoke before laughs now. "I didn't ask. We don't make it a habit of questioning the magicians. If you want to get to the next quad, get in the boat. Otherwise, you're wasting our time."

I look at Wexley, but he just shrugs at me. I sigh and walk out onto the dock, whistling for Sam. We get into the boat. I ask the dwarf who seems to be in charge, "What's your name?"

"I am Suak. Come sit with me in the bow. The rowers need the stern for their feet." Wexley and I sit in the bow, and we are soon off. There are lanterns strung at four places around the boat. The two on the bow are shielded so they don't shine in our eyes. They allow us to see a ways out over the way we are headed.

I ask, "How long will this trip be?"

Suak says, "To the docks in the next quad is about a two-hour trip."

Wexley has a satchel with him, which he opens. He pulls out meat, cheese, and bread and hands it all to me. He reaches back in and tosses a meaty bone to Sam, who catches it and then lies down to chew and gnaw.

Wexley and I eat. He has skins filled with some sort of lightly sweet drink that is tangy and takes my thirst away. When we are done, we sit back, and I feel my eyes closing. I drift off for a bit and then wake up when I don't feel any movement.

I ask, "Why are we stopped here?"

I hear two things—Sam yelps, then a splash. Suak and two of the rowers pick me up and toss me over the side, then Wexley is thrown in with us.

"This is as far as we go, Hawk Archer. Keep swimming and you should make it to the next dock in a day or so." The rowers laugh as they put oars to water and row away from us. The light grows dim. I hear Wexley spitting water. He says, "Help! I can't swim!" I hear Sam yelp again and turn to see Wexley trying to pull himself up onto Sam in the dimming light.

Sam swims away and Wexley goes under. Then the light is gone, and Wexley isn't making a sound.

Chapter Fourteen

Finding the Way

I call out, "Sam! Wexley!" I hear splashing near me and head that way. Soon I'm feeling Sam's tongue on my face. "Good boy. Find Wexley, Sam. Take me to Wexley."

Sam turns and starts swimming off. I hold to his tail and try to keep up to avoid yanking on it. Soon we stop, and I feel around. I touch hair and note that the face is under water. I pull Wexley toward me. He is limp and unmoving.

"Wexley! Answer me!" I slap his face but there is no response. He isn't moving. I put my ear close to his mouth and I can't hear him breathing. I put my hand over his heart and there is nothing. No heartbeat, no movement. I cry now as I pull Wexley to me and hug him, which is awkward when you're treading water, but I've always been a fairly good swimmer.

I often went to the lake close to the village to swim along with my friends in the village. There were few that could beat me in a swimming contest.

I say, "Wexley, please don't die." I really liked this kid. He'd had a rough time of it when his parents were down on their luck. I don't know how long he'd been a slave before I'd met him, but the time we had spent together was time I would remember fondly, despite the fact we were both slaves. Wexley is a friend, and I have never had many of those. Growing up, I was always different. The few kids I called friends all thought me strange for wanting to wander out of the village.

Now, Wexley is limp and unmoving. I weep for him. I don't know how long, but eventually I know I have to get moving. Sam won't last long; I can keep treading water for hours if I have to.

I say, "Sam, lead us back to the docks." I put an arm under Wexley's chin and start swimming alongside Sam. I can hear Sam's labored breathing and I wonder if maybe there's a chance of a beach near one of the channel walls. I start swimming at an angle to the direction Sam is going. It takes a long time, but finally I touch stone. I make myself vertical hoping that just maybe I'll be able to stand up but it's too deep. Sam has followed me to the wall and now sets off towards the docks.

We swim like this for perhaps thirty minutes when I notice Sam is struggling. I hear him breathing and then there is no sound for a few seconds before he breaths again. I reach out to him and grab him under the neck, but holding Wexley and Sam makes me go under. I surface and breath and try to pull them both along. Sam is whining now, struggling to stay above the surface.

I have to make a decision, so I let Wexley go and pull Sam onto me like I'm a raft. I lie on my back, Sam resting on my chest, and I swim slowly in the direction Sam was leading. I follow the wall.

I call out, "I'm so sorry Wexley! So sorry! I promise to come back for you no matter what. We will find you my friend and take you..." I start to say home but then remember Wexley's indifference when I suggested he could leave the mountain and head home if he wanted to. I think that maybe I was all the home he had, and that makes me weep again. I must look like a complete idiot, swimming, holding on to a dog who is totally exhausted and will drown if I don't keep him above water, and all the while crying my eyes out.

I slow my progress so that I don't tire myself to the point that I will start to fail. The added weight of Sam on my chest is comforting but requires more energy. For the first time, I start thinking that maybe we aren't going to make it. That I'm going to give up.

I think about Ma and her stew of all things. I guess food is something that sticks in the memory when we think of home. I can almost taste the potatoes, peas, and carrots plus whatever meat she had handy to put in it. I think about Ma's laugh when I joked with her. She always had a sense of humor; at least while Preacher wasn't anywhere near us.

I reach out and touch the wall. It's still there. Sam has his head on my chest and at least isn't panting as much. I'll let him ride there as long as he likes. Dogs expend a lot of energy in the water. At least I can tread water, or float on my back. Dogs are constantly moving when their feet can't touch bottom. Probably something ingrained in them.

I continue my slow strokes, moving us inch by inch, hoping I somehow make it back before I'm totally wiped out and sink into the lake along with my best friend. Thoughts of the village return, and I wonder if maybe if the vision hadn't taken me and if I'd stayed that maybe I'd have gotten married. Maybe I would have married Dahlia. She seemed to like me as much as I liked her.

My thoughts move on to Preacher and Stiggs, thoughts of revenge now forgotten, replaced with a burning anger for King Ruuc and Wuruch. I let that anger burn and give me the energy to keep going.

Sam whimpers a little and I feel him slipping. I grab him around the neck and hold on. I've lost one good friend, and I'm not about to lose another now. I slowly swim towards the docks, touching the wall every once in a while, keeping one arm around Sam to hold him up. I can feel that he's not moving his back legs now but just lying exhausted. I know that if I slip and let him go, he's not going to stay afloat for even a minute.

I continue on. I think of what I'm going to do when I reach the docks. I'm going to find a way to channel power and open up every slave collar I can feel close to me. Then I'm going to find Wuruch and Ruuc. I am going to give them to the ogres and watch them be torn apart.

They have no honor. A deal is a deal, and they broke this one and left us all for dead. Now I live for the look on their faces when they see I'm alive. I live for the image of their dying. I want their lives, and I don't care how I will get them.

I feel strong now. Anger burns through my body, surging and making me stay afloat, allowing me to move ever closer to my revenge. I hang on to Sam and swim. Time has no meaning, and the darkness is our companion. The arm holding on to Sam grows numb, and I have trouble with keeping him on my chest.

I have no sense of how far we have traveled or how long we have been in the water. Sam slides off my chest and I grab him as he struggles to keep his head up. I pull him back onto my chest and continue swimming. I can't feel my arms or legs now. I feel my lips slide below water as I'm taking a breath. Coughing and choking, I clutch Sam close.

"Sam, I think we might die out here. I don't think I can keep on much longer."

The anger still burns in me, but my body has reached the limits of its endurance. Maybe if I could just lie and rest for a bit. But as soon as I stop paddling, Sam starts to drag me down.

"No worries, Sam, I won't let go of you. If we go, we go together. I won't lose you too." I can't feel my fingers, but I clutch Sam tight. He yelps and flails and then I lose my grip. I hear him splashing and then a strange strangling noise. Sam must be sinking. I reach toward the sound but grab empty air. I dive and feel my way around, but I don't feel anything. My lungs feel like they will burst, and I go back to the surface to grab a breath.

"Sam! Sam don't leave me!"

I see a light off in the distance coming from behind us. I wonder if I'm hallucinating at first. I blink and the light doesn't flicker or suddenly disappear. It grows stronger now, and then I catch a glimpse of something floating near me. I reach out and pull Sam by the ear to me. He yelps in pain, and to me it's the best sound in the world. He's still alive. I clutch him to me and watch as the light grows stronger.

Now I can see the shape of a boat and oars plowing through the water. I yell, "Help!" but the oars don't change their rhythm or direction. I yell again, "HELP!" I try to wave, but the motion sends my head down into the water. I move my arms to bring my head back above the surface and sputter water out of my mouth, blowing it from my nose. The boat is nearly beside us now and I try one last time. "HELP! PLEASE HELP US!"

The boat stops near and the face of a dwarf peers over the edge. "We can hear you, young man. Save your breath now and we'll pull you aboard." I am out of breath as I try to laugh. I hold Sam to me as they try to grab me under the arms.

"No, get my dog first. Take Sam, then get me."

The hands obey and reach for Sam, pulling him on board the boat. I close my eyes and thank the Light. Hands reach down for me and pull me upwards from my armpits, over the side and into the boat. I lie exhausted and panting.

More dwarf faces appear above me, soft and flickering in the light of the torches placed at intervals. A collar goes around my neck, and I hear the click as it is locked in place. I don't care at this point, but later this will work in my favor. I will make it work.

"What is your name, human?"

I continue panting for a minute or so, but then reply, "I'm Hawk Archer, and this is my dog, Samuel Pettifog."

"Pettifog? Like the famous bard?"

I smile. It seems everyone knows Pettifog. I ask, "Did you see a boy in the water behind us? Did you get Wexley?"

The dwarf strokes his beard and says. "We have him yes. He wasn't as lucky as you are, but I guess you probably know that. Who are you, anyway? Runaways trying to swim your way to the other dome?"

"We were being taken to the next quadrant when our captors dumped us overboard and took off."

The one talking says, "How come we didn't see them pass us?"

I look at him. "What is your name, sir?"

"I'm Olan Fire. I am the mage on this boat. Now answer me, we saw no other boat headed for Evonne's quadrant. We picked up your friend back there, so you are headed toward Ruuc's kingdom, aren't you?"

"We were being taken to Evonne's quadrant, but then they dumped me, my friend, and Sam into the lake and turned around to head back to Ruuc's quadrant."

"Why would they do that? Whose slave are you?"

I think for a moment, not too long so as to make them think I'm coming up with a lie. I consider telling them I'm Ruuc's slave, but I don't remember seeing any slaves around him. Instead, I tell them, "I belong to Wuruch."

They all nod. Olan says, "Well, we'll just take you to him and get this sorted out, won't we?"

I don't reply but I start thinking of a plan to get Olan to zap me. I'll wait until we dock, though.

Chapter Fifteen

The End of a Culture

I can't stop staring at Wexley's body. It's lying under a white tarp in the bow of the boat. I sit against the side, my whole body vibrating with emotion and the need for some sort of justice. I touch the collar around my neck, and Olen flicks a finger at me. I feel a twinge of pain, and a small surge of power fills my fingers. I smile at Olen, and he returns a puzzled look.

I think to myself he's going to be easy. I'll just shove him or maybe call him a turd. It will take hardly anything to set him off and make him zap me.

Sam sits next to me, once again his contented dog self, eyes half closed, tongue lolling out as he pants. I envy him the seeming lack of despair and sadness. I suppose dogs get it right though. They make note of an event and then move on. Probably just as well as they don't live nearly long enough to carry regrets very far.

We come out of the tunnel, then the boat heads for the docks. There is lots of activity in the street beyond. As we pull to be tied up, Olen asks a deck handler, a troll, what is going on. "Wuruch has taken over the kingdom. King Ruuc, is dead they say."

Olen says, "How long ago did this happen?"

The troll replies, "Not long, just a few hours ago."

I feel a piece of a puzzle I hadn't known I was working on fall into place. Ruuc hadn't betrayed me—he'd been set up as well. Wuruch waited until I was gone, maybe to keep me from helping Ruuc, maybe just as a diversion. I rub my chin and step out of the boat.

Olen says, "Where do you think you're going?"

I ignore him and whistle for Sam. He jumps out of the boat, and we start up the causeway leading to the street.

Olen yells at me, and I can feel the pain from the collar. "Hey you, Hawk, I didn't give you permission to leave!" The pain is intense, but it is welcome. It overwhelms the sadness and other misery I'm feeling at the moment. Who knew physical pain was more welcome than the pain you can feel in your soul?

I stay on my feet barely, but I turn to Olen and smile. Then I flick my own fingers and he is knocked into the water along with the other dwarves. I turn to the troll. "What is your name?"

She says, "I am called Truut. You are Hawk Archer, aren't you? I've heard you can release us from the collar."

I flick a finger, and her collar clicks open and falls to the ground. I look around. "I can, and I will. Would you like to come with me and help me find my friends and Wuruch?"

Truut says, "I'm not sure I'd like that. I don't much care for violence."

"You can cover your eyes."

Truut thinks about this and then says, "You are very persuasive, Hawk Archer. I will help you."

We walk to the causeway gate, and I try to remember the phrase Dust and Sage taught me. I think now would be an appropriate time to use it. As we walk, I reach out with my newfound sense and feel for collars, opening all that I touch.

When we get to the gates, I see there is a contingent of dwarf soldiers along with the ogres. I smile at them and ask, "Do you know who I am?"

"You are Hawk Archer. We have come to take you to Wuruch."

I nod and say, "Well, I don't need all of you." I flick a finger, then all but one dwarf is thrown to the ground. I flick another finger and the collars come off the ogres and clatter to the ground. Just as Sage and Dust did, these ogres look at the collars for a moment. The standing dwarf does too but then he does something really stupid and tries to run from me. I knock him to the ground.

I check on him and the others. I want to see them smoldering and burning, but I hold myself in check. I will not become some sort of monster. What was done to me is not right, but a part of me knows that to reciprocate would be to lose my own self, my soul. I assure myself they are all breathing, and I turn to the ogres, who are rubbing their necks and eying the dwarves.

I say, *"Ach nabeknae gala."* I know that's not quite right. They all look at me, a little confused by this human who has set them free then tried to speak their language to them.

I close my eyes and try again. *"A'ach nabeknae g'la."*

They all grunt and one of them speaks. "I am Pars, friend of Sage, I will help you."

Another comes forward and says, "I am Rock, friend of Dust, I will help you."

The other four come forward and I learn that I now am friends to the first two and to Gar, Loam, Salt, and Flavor. I'm a little surprised at the one with the multisyllabic name but I suppose it might have some meaning as to this one's status. I am convinced of this when I ask, "Which of you is in charge?" Flavor takes a step toward me and says, "I lead this garden."

"Garden? What is a garden?"

"We are." Flavor points at the others.

"Why do some of you have plant names and some have dirt or rock names?"

"Plant names for women, dirt names for men."

I say, "I need to find Wuruch, can you help me?"

Flavor shrugs. "We don't know where to find him."

Truut says, "You don't need them to help you, I can find Wuruch. He will be in the palace most likely."

There is white hot pain emanating from my collar. I grit my teeth and turn to see a dwarf mage gesturing towards me. He is with a contingent of ogres. I briefly wonder how long they will continue to use their slaves as guards. I flick a finger and the mage goes flying back, landing hard on the ground, hitting his head. I flick another finger and the collars come off the ogre guards. They all stand looking down at the collars.

I say, "Flavor, can you explain to these ogres what we are doing? Truut, lead the way please."

We start towards the street. The ogres all gather together, the new contingent still rubbing their necks as if they expect to feel the collar there. As they talk, Truut leads me out to the street, with Sam trotting beside me. When we get to the intersection, I say, "Truut, wait here for a moment and let the ogres catch up."

I close my eyes. I can sense the collars around me easier with my eyes closed for some reason. I reach out and unlock close to a hundred collars. Intense pain again shoots up into my head, white and loud, but I stay on my feet and look around, trying to locate the mage who is zapping me.

He's two streets down, but his hand gestures give him away. I flick and he goes soaring backwards into a wall. He slides down and lands in a limp heap. I get control of myself and decide I'd better use less of the power. I really don't want to kill anyone. Well, anyone except Wuruch, but that piece of dung deserves death for what he's done.

The ogres have caught up to us now and I say, "Lead us to the palace, Truut."

As we walk, I decide to try and find out more about ogres. "Flavor, how long did it take for you to learn our language?"

She grunts, "Ogres learn language easy. I know we look stupid to other kinds, but we not. We just slow in our thinking. We know all languages we spend time with."

"That's good to know. Will you return to your home when we are done here?"

She shrugs, "I think most of us will. I haven't decided yet, Hawk Archer."

I think I might have a use for someone who knows languages at some point. So far, the people I've met all speak versions close to my own. Close enough that it's no trouble communicating.

I ask, "Where are you from?"

"From the hill country north of the mountain. We are herders—sheep, cows, pigs, that sort of thing."

We turn a corner and run into a small army of dwarf troops. They have a mage with them who raises his hands and I feel the white pain again. I throw them all down to the ground.

Flavor says, "Maybe you could leave some for us next time."

I laugh. "Yes, I'll do that."

Flavor isn't laughing. I see that she's serious.

I say, "I didn't mean to offend or anything."

"You not know, so no offense. But we ogres have pride in our combat. You let us help, yes?"

"Yes, I let you help."

Truut has led us to a main thoroughfare. I reach out and hear hundreds of clicks and clatter as collars fall. Soon there is some chaos as former slaves run or turn and attack their dwarf mages. Truut calmly leads us across the thoroughfare to a giant gleaming building of multiple colors. As we approach, I see that the colors come from varied gemstones embedded in the granite used to construct the palace.

I say, "Wow, there's enough gems here to make the entire quadrant rich."

Truut nods and says, "There is the entrance. With the change in leadership and the commotion you are causing, Hawk, there will be extra guards there." She points to a large gate that seems made from heavy wrought iron.

I look up at Flavor. "Can you take down the gate, or would you like me to?"

Another mage somewhere hits me with power. The surge glows from my fingers. I'm not sure what the upper limit is to this power in me, but I think it's enough that I should be scared of using it. I push the mage on to his back. I reach out and more collars clatter to the ground.

Former slaves are running here and there, most of them headed for the gates leading out of the city into the open plains.

Flavor and her Garden approach the gate. There are both dwarf and ogre guards there, but the ogres are touching their necks and staring at the dwarves. Flavor grabs a part of the gate and wrenches it backwards. The other ogres all do the same and soon there's an opening big enough for them to get through.

Before they enter, the ogre guards have beaten the dwarf guards. I see a lot of blood. I can control only what I do, I think. I can't be responsible for what the slaves do to their former masters.

We enter and Truut says, "Your friends will be in the sub-basement where the cages are kept. Wuruch will be in the tower there." She points to the highest point in the complex. I think to myself it might be a great vantage point, but it is also a trap waiting to be sprung. There is nowhere to go but down from that tower.

I turn to the ogres. "I should go find my friends. Can you make your way up that tower and grab Wuruch?"

Flavor nods and speaks in ogreish to her companions. They head for the tower. I say to Truut, "Do you think you can find the cages?"

Truut says, "I know I can. I've spent enough time in them." She leads me to an entrance, and we pass through gleaming white walls to a courtyard. She passes through it. I notice smallish beings with large ears and shaggy hair. Their ears are tufted with gray hairs, and they have large blue eyes.

I say, "Hello." I release them from their collars.

One of them says, "You are Hawk Archer. It's good to meet you. You can call me Sprout."

"Well met, Sprout. Are you a dwarf?"

Sprout laughs. "We are gnomes. We work the palace gardens."

"Well, now you may return to your homes if you wish."

Sprout shrugs. "Most of us were born here in the palace. Most of us have parents and grandparents who were born here. This is our home."

I think there is going to be a need for some sort of leadership for the former slaves. I hadn't thought much about that, since I was so new to it. For those that had never known anything but slavery, it might be hard to transition to freedom.

Truut leads me to a corridor on the other side of the courtyard and up to a large wooden door encased with metal and with handles of black iron. I reach out to touch it when I am hit with what feels like a thousand lightning bolts. It's enough to send me to my knees. I fight to keep from passing out and turn just enough to see a dozen mages all focusing on me.

Dots of white light float in front of me, and my eyesight is growing dim. I struggle to stay focused, but the intensity of the pain tells me they don't much care if they kill me. In fact, I think that is exactly what they are trying to do.

Chapter Sixteen

Reunited

I hear Sam barking and before I can black out, I see him rush the mob of mages. It's enough to distract several of them, and the power hitting me lessens enough that I am able to throw back at them and toss them all to the ground. Truut and I wander over to them.

I say, "I can't leave them here. When they come to, they will just chase me down and try again. They almost succeeded this time." I think to myself that they will also come up with a way to get rid of Sam if there's a next time.

I look over to where the gnomes are touching their necks and staring at the dozen mages on the ground.

I call out, "Sprout, do you think you can help me? I need rope and material I can use to gag these mages."

Sprout blinks and seems unsure, but then she nods to me. "I will get what you ask for, Hawk." She gestures to the other gnomes, and they walk towards a shed at the side of the gardens. I walk with Truut over to where the mages are knocked out cold. I reach down and ruffle Sam's fur. "Good boy Sam! Well done."

I bend so Sam can lick my face, then I check to make sure all the mages really are knocked out. I hear one of them groan. He tries to sit up, but I zap him lightly. He falls back to the ground.

The gnomes return, all carrying rope or patches of white cloth.

"Truut, can you tie knots that these mages won't be able to get out of?"

"Of course, Hawk." She takes rope from one of the gnomes and begins tying up a mage.

"No, roll him on his stomach and tie his hands behind his back. It makes it harder for them to get loose if they can't see the knot."

Truut says, "But Hawk, the mage behind him will have a clear view of the knot."

I think about this. I decide it's still better if the knot is behind their back.

"The mage behind won't be able to work the knot if their hands are tied."

Truut seems to see the light in this, so rolls her dwarf onto his stomach and ties his hands.

I say, "Once we have them all tied and gagged, we will tie them together front to back."

I wonder if I should really be taking the time to do all this. I keep watching the entrances to the garden, but no one is coming. I bet most of the palace guard is trying to calm the chaos in the streets. I close my eyes and feel more collars. I release them all and get back to tying up the mages. Once we have them all bound, gagged, and tied together, I slap the one in the lead. He blinks and glares up at me. He tries to speak, but his gag prevents any understandable speech.

"Come on, on your feet." I haul him vertical, then do the same with the next in line. Between Truut and myself, we have them all standing up in less than a minute.

"Okay folks, on to the dungeons!"

I grab a rope I've tied to the lead mage and tug on it. He stumbles forward and soon we are all walking towards the heavy wooden door. I blast it with energy, and it blows open, splintering and sending pieces in every direction. We are far enough away that none of them get close enough to harm us. I stop and gesture to Truut. She comes forward and I hand her the rope for the lead mage.

"Take us to the cages. Have you seen my friends down there?"

"I know where they are." She takes the rope from me and goes through the door, tugging the lead dwarf. I take up the rear with Sam and follow, watching behind to see if anyone will try to attack and watching the dwarves in front of me for any sign that they are trying to free themselves.

Truut steps carefully over the debris. I follow and find myself inside an entrance room. There is a guard station at one end, but it's deserted. I can see three collars on the ground, which is all I need to know what happened. I reach out but can find no additional collars here.

Truut leads us past the guard station and into a series of corridors. Truut doesn't hesitate but takes a passageway on the left side. We all follow, Sam stopping to sniff here and there, in doggy heaven with lots of new scents to be sniffed, I suppose.

The corridor leads to an intersection. We can either turn left or right—Truut takes the right turn, and we continue down another corridor. It's dark in here, and the covered torches are the only light now. We travel perhaps three hundred meters until we come to another guard station. Again, there are a few collars on the ground but no ogres present.

"Are we close now, Truut?"

Truut responds, "Just through this door and to the left."

I hear a voice. "Hello? Hawk, is that you?" It's Grain. It's a welcome sound but also one that brings the apprehension of having to share bad news. We go left and there are several cages with prisoners in them. One holds Grain, and another holds Chortnel.

"Hello friends! I'm back," I say.

Chortnel says, "It's good to see you, Hawk."

I say, "Truut, meet my friends Chortnel and Grain."

Truut nods. "Yes, it is good to meet you. I was in this prison for quite a while. I know how bad things can get."

Several of the prisoners start talking all at once. I raise my hands, but they don't stop. Finally, I yell, "Please, let me speak."

They grow quiet. I say, "If you would all please turn your backs and get as far from your door as possible, I'm going to open them for you." I turn to Truut. "Can you go find cages for these dwarves? I don't want to have to cart them around all over the palace."

"Of course, Hawk, I'll take care of them."

I say, "Try to put them all in separate cages instead of all together." Truut leads the mages away.

Grain is standing with her back to me on the wall opposite her door. I flick power at the locking mechanism, and it blows apart. The door creaks open. Sam whines a bit and I ruffle his head. "Sam, go with Truut, help her with the prisoners."

Sam licks my hand, then turns and bounds off in the direction Truut went. A dog's ears are sensitive, and I'm sure the loud noise of the exploding locks must be painful for him.

I turn back to the next cage; it holds two elves that look similar to Grain. They also have their backs to me. I blast the lock and their door opens. I continue around the cages until they are all open. Grain hugs me, then Chortnel hugs me as well. Her baby is further out of her shoulder now, but still not completely free.

I ask her, "How much longer for the little one to be born?"

"Soon, I think. She is making me itch night and day now."

As if to demonstrate, Chortnel scratches her left shoulder.

"Okay, I need to go find Wuruch and take care of him. Anyone who wants to go with me is welcome, otherwise you are all on your own now. You can return to your homes or whatever you choose."

There's a sound coming from down the corridor. It's a sort of muffled wail. I go to investigate, walking down the corridor. Most of the prisoners follow me, Chortnel and Truut right behind me and Sam. Sam runs down the corridor and barks in front of one of the cages. When I catch up, I see King Ruuc inside, his mouth gagged and his hands tied.

I look him over and say, "They really wanted to make sure you didn't escape, didn't they?" He says something but it's muffled. I add, "Turn around and get as far from the door as you can."

There's a voice behind me. "That won't be necessary, I've got the keys." At the rear of our little group is an elf holding up a brass ring with several keys on it.

I say, "Great, do you know which one opens this door?"

The elf replies, "No, but it has to be one of these."

There must be two dozen keys on the ring at least. I say, "Never mind that. Ruuc, do as I say, turn around and get as far from the door as you can." He turns and shuffles over to the far corner. I send power at the lock, and it explodes. The door creaks open. I go inside and try to undo the knots on the king's hands.

Chortnel steps up beside me and says, "Here, let me try that, you get his gag off."

I reach up to the cloth tied around the king's mouth and get it undone.

Ruuc says, "Thank the Light you are alive, Hawk Archer. I thought I'd die without ever seeing you again."

I said, "I lost my friend, and nearly died out there on the lake, but there was a boat headed this way. They picked me up."

Grain said, "What about Wexley? Why isn't he with you?"

I shake my head. "They threw us in the water, and it got dark quick when the boat left. Wexley couldn't swim and he panicked. He nearly drowned Sam trying to stay afloat. Before I could reach him, he drowned."

Grain and Chortnel let out breaths. Chortnel said, "He was a good lad."

Grain said, "He was my friend."

I nodded. "He was a good friend and a good person. He didn't deserve to die, but there was nothing I could do." I can feel tears coming so I add, "But we have business yet. Wuruch will pay for what he's done."

Ruuc says, "He will have a lot of guards."

I hear a voice from behind us. "How right you are, Ruuc. I do have a lot of guards."

I turn around and look directly into Wuruch's eyes. I can feel the anger building in me. He has the ogres back in collars. I chide myself for not checking around me. But I hadn't found any collars the last two times I'd checked.

Wuruch says, "Put a collar on the king, Flavor."

Flavor steps forward, but I'm not having it this time. I can feel the anger build, cold and hot at the same time, burning white, icy, hot anger and hatred.

I say quietly, my eyes never leaving Wuruch's eyes, "I can't let you do that, Flavor."

Wuruch smiles at me. "You want me to kill your new friends, Hawk? You want to be responsible for their deaths?"

I say, "There is one person here who is responsible for the death of my friend, Wuruch. Wexley was a kind person who never hurt you or anyone else in life. He never had much in the way of luck, and he was still ten times the better man then you could ever hope to be."

Wuruch grimaces. "Careful, Hawk." Flavor drops onto the floor, writhing in agony, I search for her collar, to release her from the pain, but I can't spot it. I'm looking right at it, but the power in me doesn't see what my eyes see. Then I notice it is the color of silver, or white gold.

I ask, "What have you done, Wuruch? Why can't I touch these new collars?"

Wuruch laughs, and another of the ogres drops to the floor, writhing in pain. "Give up, Hawk. Give me your collar and I won't kill your friends."

I have had enough of all this. "You know, Wuruch, when I started on this quest, I was just a curious boy seeking to find the world. But you have changed me. I'm no longer just that boy looking for innocent fun."

I look up at him as he pulls down another ogre, one I brought to him as a friend. One more I had thought I could protect.

"You stop now, Wuruch." I reach out and throw him back against the wall, pinning him in white searing bolts of energy. I am the lightning, and I shoot through him until he begins to dissolve. He melts there against the wall. I pour enough energy into him that even his bones dissolve. All that is left when I am done is a dark smear in the shape of a dwarf. A shadow where there had been a life.

The collars around the ogres and others Wuruch had shackled fall away as he dies. I have won. I exacted justice and took my revenge.

Then I fall to my knees and get sick. I retch up whatever meager contents I have in my stomach as I contemplate what I might become with the power I now have.

I am tired. The world is spotty and unfocused. I hear Chortnel calling me. I feel Sam's tongue on my cheek, but neither is enough to keep me awake. I fall into the darkness and the bliss of feeling nothing.

Chapter Seventeen

The Aftermath

I wake up with a headache. This time it's not quite so overpowering as after a vision. I must have expended too much energy on Wuruch, and it just drained me. The thought of Wuruch and what I did to him puts a bitter taste in my mouth. I am now a killer. I have taken the life of someone deliberately.

This realization makes me afraid deep in my core, in my soul. If I can get mad enough to kill once, I can do it again. I resolve to make sure the next time will not be any easier than the first. I think that going forward I must not use this power unless I absolutely have to.

I sit up and groan. I hear Grain's voice.

"So, you're awake. You've been sleeping for hours. How do you feel?"

"Groggy, but not as bad as after a vision. I just feel a bit drained."

Grain says, "Are you up for traveling? I think we should get out of here as soon as we can."

"Why? What's going on?"

Chortnel comes in, Sam following her, and says, "You're awake. Hawk."

Sam comes over to me, tail wagging. I pat his head. "Hello, best friend." I bend down and let him lick my face. I look back at Chortnel. "Grain says we should leave as soon as we can."

Chortnel nods. "The city is at war. There are slaves rebelling and two different factions trying to gain power."

I ask, "Where is Ruuc?"

Chortnel says, "He left with some guards to go to another part of the palace. I hear that he has fortified it."

"Can we get to the docks? Will there be any dwarfs to help us leave?"

Chortnel is about to reply when some of the former slaves I recognize as being there when I killed Wuruch come into the room. One of them is the elf who had the keys to the cages.

He says, "Lord Hawk, we need your help." He moves closer. "The king and the council are at war with each other. If you will help us, we can take over the city and make sure no one is ever made a slave again."

I shake my head. "I'm sorry, but that is not my fight. I have a quest to fulfill, and I have been delayed far too long already. What is your name? I remember you; you had the keys to the cages, right?"

"Yes, I did. My name is Dolain."

"Dolain, you don't need to call me Lord, I'm not royalty, okay? As to your fight for the city, I wish you well, but I have my own problems and a quest to complete."

"How will you find oarsmen? Only the dwarves know this skill and can find the way through the lake tunnel."

I think about this. Finding the way through the tunnel won't be hard; it's straightforward, as I remember. Finding skilled oarsmen might be a problem, but how hard can it be? I look to Grain, Chortnel, and Truut. "Do you think we can find enough people to go with us to use the oars?"

They all look at each other, then Chortnel says, "I don't know, Hawk, I sort of thought it would only be you, me, and Grain that will go. I suppose we could ask for help. There are a dozen ogres that haven't left the palace yet."

"If they are coordinated enough to man the oars. I don't think it takes a lot of skill, but it does have to be done as a team."

Dolain says, "It's much harder than it looks. If you have six people who have never rowed before, it will be very difficult to move the boat."

"We will deal with that when we come to it. It's time to continue my quest." I stand up, and my head feels a little dizzy. I sway a little. Grain comes over to support me. She says, "Maybe you should rest a little before we take off."

I don't want to stay here any longer than I have to. I need to get going. I say, "I'll sleep once we're on the boat and on our way. Chortnel and Truut, will you come with me?"

Chortnel scratches her shoulder and says, "Yes, Hawk, I am with you."

Truut looks at me but doesn't reply right away.

I say, "Truut, it's up to you. I don't want you to do anything you aren't ready to do. If you wish to stay and help your people, that is a good thing. It is your decision to make."

Truut says, "I am open to an adventure, Hawk Archer, I think that I want to go. I was thinking that we don't have to use the lake passage. If we go to the other quadrant, the southwest one, we can use the walking tunnel. It will take a little longer, but we won't need people to work the oars."

I nod. "Yes, that sounds like a good plan, but the northeast quadrant is where I think I need to go. The vision was leading me to a tunnel in the Dome, and Ruuc seemed to think it led to the same place as the lake passage."

Truut says, "Okay then, we go to the docks and try to find dwarves to help us with the boat."

"First, let's talk to the ogres."

Truut leads me to another area of the dungeon. I hope that the garden that came with me is among them, but I can always use the phrase Dust and Sage taught me. I don't have to wait long, as one of them comes forward. "I'm Flavor. Do you remember me Hawk?"

"Of course. Why are you here?"

"We were waiting for you. I figure you want to take the lake passage to the next quadrant. We also want to go that way. I think we can help each other."

I say, "Thanks Flavor, your help will be greatly appreciated. Do you know how to operate the oars on the boats?"

"We have never done it, but we all have watched the dwarf rowers. I think we can manage it."

We find our way out the way we came in. The garden is deserted, with no gnomes to be seen. I head to the main gate when I hear a familiar voice. "Hawk Archer! This way. Don't go to the gate."

I turn and see Sprout gesturing to us. I walk over to see what this is about. When I get close, I ask, "What is wrong at the main gate? Don't the former slaves control the palace?"

Sprout nods. "For now, they control this gate. The other faction is trying to take it, and Ruuc's force holds the other side. Both dwarf factions want the palace, but they don't want to work together to take it. If you go out there, one or the other faction will take you and your friends."

I don't see that as a major problem, but then I don't want to use my power if I don't really have to. "Okay, you can help us find a way out?"

"Come with me. I will lead you out."

I look at the others. Truut and Chortnel nod to me. Grain doesn't say anything but bites her lip. Dolain doesn't look at me, but starts following Sprout. Soon there are a dozen gnomes also following us.

Dolain asks, "Where are you taking us?"

"There are secret passages built in ancient times for forgotten kings. They were used in times of siege to escape the palace."

I ask, "Will they take us near the docks?"

Dolain says, "You will have to walk a ways, but they will be near enough that it won't take you more than an hour." He turns and looks at me. "Unless you encounter opposition, that is." He moves closer to me and speaks in a whisper, "I don't understand why gnomes are helping us. Normally they are prone to stick to their own kind and avoid contact with other peoples."

I'm not sure I know what to do with that information, but I say, "We will have to keep our eyes on them."

Soon we are led to a small forest of evergreens. The path through is lined with pine needles gone brown and red. The gnomes slip between the trees, and when we have gone about 500 meters, the path stops and disappears. We are standing in a small clearing surrounded by trees and the scent of the evergreens. It seems peaceful here, a place to come and think about one's problems maybe. I wish I had time to sit and rest, but we need to get going.

"Where is the passageway?" I ask.

A small army of dwarves comes out of the woods. They surround us, and each holds a pike pointed in our direction. There are a dozen mages (the same dozen, I wonder?) all pointing at me, but the pain from the collar is diminished. I don't feel the overwhelming white-hot feeling that comes with the magic user's aiming their power at me. I raise my hand, but it won't obey. I try to raise my other hand, but it won't obey me. I try to step forward, but my legs won't work. I don't feel any different, but my limbs refuse to do what I want them to. It's a very strange feeling.

"You won't be able to move, Hawk," says one of the mages. "The rest of you put on a collar. We have someone I need you to talk to."

I'm not going to be delayed any more. With my mind, I reach out with the new sense the magic has given me. Instead of feeling for collars, I feel for the magic coming from the mages holding me. I can sense them there, where their power is. I start to grab on to that place in each of them.

The one who spoke says again, "All of you pick up a collar and put it on."

There's a small pile of the new type of collars in front of the mages. They gleam white. I know I won't be able to touch them with my power. The ogres don't wait for a reply—they start rushing towards the mages. A dozen dwarf soldiers with pikes come out of the trees and step in front of the mages. They begin stabbing at the ogres. I see Flavor take a pike in the belly. She grabs the weapon and lifts the owner off the ground, then flings him into a tree. Another ogre goes down to the ground, stabbed in the heart. A dwarf soldier loses his pike when one of the ogres pulls it out of his grasp. I see about half the ogres have wounds, and half the dwarf soldiers are now weaponless.

One of the mages grabs a collar and puts it around Flavor's neck. She falls to the ground, writhing. I reach out with my mind and that mage explodes in white hot energy. I didn't mean to do that. I don't want to kill anyone else. I just meant to toss the mage back into the rest of them.

Everyone near the mage is now covered in blood. Flavor's collar drops off and she grabs the nearest soldier and tosses him against a tree. The mages are stunned by what happened, but only for an instant.

Three of them run off as the rest turn to me. I can see the fear in their eyes. They raise their hands above their heads.

"We give up, please don't hurt us. We are done."

I am relieved by this. I would use the power again only if it looked like we were losing, but I am glad that now I won't have to. I really need to figure a way to control it before I use it again. Killing is not an option I want to continue using.

The ogres surround the whole group. Truut asks, "Who are you working with?"

I pick up one of the gleaming white collars. I think maybe this might be a solution. Maybe these can help me control the power. I slip off the copper collar and put the white gold one around my neck. It clicks in place. I notice one of the mages looking interested in what I'm doing. He flicks a finger, and I can feel the pain turning into power. I flick back, as lightly as I can. The mage goes flying back and hits a tree. I can hear something break and he slides to the ground.

Grain runs over to him and checks on him. She looks up at me and shakes her head. Another death I've caused with this damn power. The collar seems to have only increased the amount of energy rather than giving me more control. I try to take the collar off, but it won't unlatch.

The group of mages that is left seem to come to the same conclusion together. They all concentrate on me again and I can feel the power building in the collar. It's causing me more and more pain. It builds until I feel like I'm looking into a white-hot smithy furnace, so bright it hurts my eyes.

I won't kill again, I resolve. I grab the collar with my hands and try to wrench it off me, but the light and the pain grow so intense that once again, I am sent into dark oblivion.

Chapter Eighteen

The Factions

I'm staring up at a ceiling painted with naked women riding horses but with men's torsos where their neck and heads should be. They have arms, and each has a bow with an arrow nocked and ready. The women look fierce and carry bows as well, quivers slung over their shoulders. Each of the dozen or so holds an arrow knocked and ready but not yet aimed. I wonder at why they don't have any armor on. They are all lovely to look at—maybe that is why the artist didn't give them clothes?

I sit up and rub my eyes, then place my feet on the floor. I'm in a large room, lit by torchlight. I look behind me, and the seven mages who didn't die or flee are watching me. I feel my neck and the collar is there. I can't see if it's copper or white gold, but I'm guessing it's the latter as I can't seem to unlatch it.

One of the mages looks to his left and nods. I hear footsteps, then a tall, for a dwarf anyway, person comes into the room. The eyes are different from the other dwarves I have met. I'm not sure why until I hear the dwarf speak. "I hope you have rested well, Hawk Archer."

The voice is definitely one that belongs to a woman, despite the white flowing beard.

I ask, "Where am I? Where are my friends?"

The woman dwarf says, "You don't ask who I am?"

I rub my eyes and look at her. "Okay, who are you?"

She says, "I am Jasmine, mayor of this city, head of the king's council."

I begin to put pieces together. Jasmine leads the opposition. The faction of dwarves fighting against Ruuc.

"Okay Jasmine, you know what I can do, right? I could kill you and all your friends if I chose to." I don't tell her that I wouldn't choose to do that, but she doesn't need to know everything.

Jasmine has a slight smile. "I do know that. So let me answer the second of your questions. Your friends are on a boat headed to the next quadrant. The one you want to go to for your quest or whatever it is."

"So, do I get to join them?"

"You will join them, but in order for them to stay alive, I need you to refrain from killing any of my people. If you kill one of mine, then one of yours dies. Do you understand?"

I swallow and nod. "What is it you want me to do?"

"That leads us to your first question. You are near the palace, on the side that Ruuc holds. What I want you to do is get us through the gates and help us capture Ruuc."

"You want control of the city. What about the former slaves?"

Jasmine says, "I'm already negotiating with them. I hope to come to some sort of agreement there before we capture Ruuc."

"What sort of agreement are you going to make with them?"

"Those that want to stay will work for me, not as slaves, but as paid workers. The rest will be allowed to leave and go home to wherever it was they came from."

I ask, "You will stop making the collars?"

Jasmine nods. "We won't have any need for slave collars if there are no slaves."

It occurs to me that her words require a lot of trust on my part. I try to think of a way to verify what she is telling me is true. I think about Flavor and Dolain. I say, "I want to speak to the former slaves, especially any that I know."

"I can bring you Sprout. She's out in the forest with her gnomes."

"No, Sprout has been working with you. She led me into the trap, didn't she? No, there was an elf named Dolain and a garden of ogres led by Flavor. Let me speak with any of them."

"Why do you want to speak to them?"

"I want to be sure they are okay and that this negotiation you tell me about is real."

She starts pacing, her hands behind her back. "You want to know if I'm lying to you."

"If you want to put it that way, yes."

"If I am lying, you still don't know where your friends are or if they are safe. What difference will it make? Either you help us and I will get you transport to the next quadrant to meet up with your friends, or you don't help us and I still get your transport, only there will be a boat leaving before you do, and by the time you arrive, all there will be is corpses."

I say, "You are asking me for my help, but do you understand what that means? You know I've killed two of your mages and Wuruch. The only help I can give you is more death. I can't control my power. If I use it, people die."

Jasmine stops pacing and laughs lightly. "Well then, you had best be sure the deaths are the right deaths."

I hope that isn't true. I will have to find a way to make it true. I have three deaths riding on my soul, and that is weight enough.

I say, "What is your plan?"

Jasmine says, "Ruuc is holding the north gate. My plan is to enter the palace from the south gate if negotiations go well with the former slaves. Once we are inside the palace grounds, it will be easier to defeat Ruuc's forces."

"What if the former slaves don't agree to terms?"

"Then we will attack the north gate and, with your help, gain entry that way."

I try to find a way out of this. If Jasmine is telling me the truth, then there really isn't a way out that I can see except to go along with her plans. If she's lying to me, and my friends are already dead or being held somewhere else...

But I don't think she would risk that. She seems to be a smart person, and smart people don't take unnecessary risks. She has heard of the power I have and the people I've killed already. I don't think she'd risk me finding out my friends were already killed or are imprisoned somewhere here in the kingdom. It makes sense that what she is telling me is the truth.

"Then let's go meet these former prisoners and go from there."

The seven mages surround me as we begin following Jasmine and her guard through corridors. It looks like we are underground somewhere, and that is confirmed when we come to a staircase leading up onto a large street above. There are a few people moving about, but mostly the large thoroughfare is deserted. I am again struck by the magnificence of this city. Buried under a mountain, the buildings are carved into the mountain itself, and the roads leading up to each tier are carefully constructed with rock rims to keep travelers from falling off the road's edge. But the most spectacular thing about this city are the jewels. Everywhere you look there are the vibrant colors encrusted into the buildings and even into the roads. It's a sight I will never forget, but I will also associate it with my friend Wexley, his small life never a very good one yet he remained good and kind. He didn't deserve what they did to him. I suppose no one really does, but Wexley less than most.

Jasmine turns and begins walking down the wide street. I can see the palace in the distance, gleaming white and multi-colored with the jewels embedded in patterns I don't recognize. We walk for perhaps a half kilometer to the gate I'd entered into the palace before. There are ogres on duty at the gate, and I wait to see if any recognize me. I have trouble telling them apart and could be looking right at Flavor or one of her garden mates and not know it.

Jasmine stops and addresses the ogres. "You know who I am and why I am here."

The one standing in front of the others nods. "Wait here, Dolain will guide you in a moment." Dolain, the elf I had first met when he had a set of keys for the cages under the palace, arrives with three more ogres. One of the ogres nods to me and says, "Hello Hawk, do you remember me?"

I say, "I have trouble remembering ogre faces, but I'll know your name if we've met before."

The ogre says, "I am Salt from Flavor's Garden."

"Is your Garden all doing well?"

"Thank you for asking. We are well."

Dolain comes and greets me. "Hello, Hawk, it's good to see you again."

I take his hand. "It's good to see you as well, Dolain."

Dolain turns to Jasmine. "You, Hawk, one mage, and one soldier may follow me."

Jasmine hesitates. "I will need all my mages with me."

Dolain shakes his head. "Hawk, I trust you won't use your power while we discuss things?"

I look at Dolain and then at Jasmine. "I will refrain from using it. I promise."

Jasmine doesn't look convinced, but she must realize that she won't be able to have her way on this. She says, "That's fine. Mason and Loam, you will come with us." She turns to Dolain and waits. Dolain leads us away from the gate and into the palace.

Once inside, we see a table has been set. On the other side sit Truut and Flavor along with elves, ogres, and other people I don't recognize. On our side of the table sit three dwarves. They stand and bow to Jasmine when we enter.

Dolain says, "Please sit. Would you care for drink or food?"

We all politely decline. We sit facing the former slaves.

Dolain says, "I think it's safe to say we can dispense with the small talk. Your representatives and I have come to a possible agreement."

One of the dwarves grunts and nods to Jasmine. She acknowledges him and turns back to Dolain. "Go on then, I'm listening."

"We, the former slaves, agree to help you in taking back the palace and the city. We will fight for you and pledge our allegiance to you once the city is in your hands. In exchange, we want an office created that answers to me and me alone, that will be responsible for the destruction of all slave collars and the punishing of anyone who makes or uses one of them."

Jasmine nods. "I can accept that. What else?"

"There will be a council formed of the workers in the city. The council will accept all races, dwarf included, and negotiate with you or your designated representative for the terms of our work agreements with you and the city."

Jasmine says, "That sounds like an issue for my council to look over. Will you accept a tentative agreement until a full council can be sworn in and hold court?"

Dolain looked to his friends. They whisper to each other for a minute, then Dolain replies, "As long as you recognize our right to refuse to work should we not be able to come to an agreement."

Jasmine squirms a little. "So you want some sort of contract outlining duties and rights and things like that?"

I yawn. I don't have a stake in what is going on here. I just want to get on to the next bit and take the palace away from Ruuc.

Jasmine continues, "I agree to your terms. Can we plan our invasion now?"

Dolain says, "The invasion has already begun. We have people placed in secret all over the palace. Our people know the halls and secret passages of the place far better than any dwarf does. All we need you to do is get through the main gate. Once Ruuc commits most of his defense there, we will swoop in from behind him and take control."

Jasmine taps me on the shoulder. "Should be easy enough with the lightning mage on our side."

Dolain smiles. 'We've been calling him the Wizard of Fire."

I'm not sure I should keep either name. I don't feel important enough, and certainly the power I have is not something I should be praised for. It isn't like I asked for it, or even trained hard to use. It was forced on me, like a slave collar.

We break from meeting, then I follow Jasmine, who is conferring with her mages. I hear a little bit of what she is saying, something about hiding something. I don't like this. If she is being deceitful with the former slaves, it is not going to turn out well.

Nothing is going to turn out well if these people keep stabbing each other in the back. They walk out of the palace and back to the headquarters Jasmine is using. She says to me, "Come, we have plans to make!"

Chapter Nineteen

King Ruuc

I catch up to Jasmine. "Jasmine, how will you know it's time to attack the gate?"

Jasmine looks at me strangely. "Didn't you hear us discussing that?"

I say, "I sort of quit listening."

"I'm sorry the fate of our city bores you. But to your question, the former slaves are all ready and just waiting for the explosion to come out of their hiding places and capture King Ruuc."

I think they must be really great hiding places if ogres can stay hidden in them. "So, you are going back for your army and then we go?" I'm anxious to get this all over with. I really want to put this entire place behind me as quick as I can without hurting anyone else.

We walk in silence for a while. I think about when I was just a kid wandering around the outskirts of the village, and then going a little further as I grew older. I didn't have to worry about anything then. It was just me and Sam exploring the world and having a great time doing it.

Now, here I am, a powerful wizard sought by the most powerful people in a kingdom far away from my village and my Ma. I know I can't go back there, but it's nice to think about those days. Ma scolding me when I'd come back just before the lights turned off. The smell of her pies, the warmth of our home.

I'm taken out of my reverie by a group of dwarf soldiers that rounds a corner. I think everyone is surprised.

Jasmine asks, "Who are you?"

A dwarf in a colorful suit with lots of ribbons on his chest steps forward. "I am General Prate, the King's advisor." He flicks a finger and I brace for the pain, but instead the general's soldiers fan out and surround us.

Prate says, "I think you are Mayor Jasmine, aren't you?"

Jasmine strokes her beard. "You must be new, general, I don't recall ever meeting a Prate in the service of the king."

Prate doesn't respond to that but says, "You will come with us to the king. I believe he's very interested in talking to you."

Jasmine squeezes my shoulder. "Do you know who this is, general?"

I don't like the touch of her hand on me. I step away so her hand falls from my shoulder.

Prate says, "Let's see, human boy, brown skin, one of those new slave collars around his neck. This must be the Fire Wizard."

Several of Prate's soldiers surround me now, the points of their pikes just inches from me. I say, "General sir, I have no argument with you. I don't want to hurt you or anyone. If you will just let us pass, I promise you that you will be safe."

The general laughs. "I have mages with me." He gestures, then six dwarves come forward and start to send power at the collar. I can feel the pain, but I don't respond. I just let the power flow from the collar down into my fingers.

But I can't let this continue too long. I'll black out eventually. I'm tired of blacking out. I am tired of waking up not knowing what happened or where I am. Most of all, I'm tired of dwarves and their grumpy ways. They always believe they have the upper hand. I concentrate on the paving in front of the wizard dwarves, and just then Jasmine signals her troops. They begin fighting. Some go after the wizards just as I send power into the ground.

I do my best to send just a little bit at the road surface. I simply want to get their attention and startle them into letting go the power. But, just like the other times, there is a large explosion and stuff goes flying. Pieces of roadway shower on the mages and soldiers alike. I curse myself. I just can't get the amount of power right. Maybe there is no right amount. Maybe any power I use now is going to be too much.

There is a cloud of smoke, and when it clears, I see a small crater in the road. On the other side the mages are on the ground, staring wide-eyed at me. I don't see any that are knocked out or, Light help me, look dead.

The same for the soldiers. I thank the Light for the favor of not killing anyone this time. I vow to myself I will not use the power again so near to people. I am not a killer. I tell myself that again and again. I am not a killer. I believe that in the depths of my being, but there is still that small kernel deep down that worries me. This power is so easy to use and so overwhelming. I tamp down on that thought, that emotion.

I say, "Is everyone okay?"

Jasmine brushes off her clothes. "Maybe you could try only using a small amount of your power?"

I reply, "I thought I was, but it always comes out like this, just a huge amount."

Jasmine says, "Maybe it's the collar. The white gold may affect your power."

She is probably right. I'd put the white gold on because I thought it would let me capture more power in. Of course, it must work the other way as well, releasing more power than I normally would. I mentally kick myself for not thinking of that sooner.

"I will need one of your mages to take the collar off. I can't seem to get it to unlock."

Jasmine gestures to the mages, and one of them comes over to us. Jasmine says, "Meraan, can you take this collar off of Hawk?"

"Yes, of course I can." He looks at the collar, moves it around on my neck, and then I hear a click and it's off.

I say, "Thank you, Meraan." I turn to Jasmine. "I may run out of power without a collar. I was storing it up whenever one of the mages sent pain into it."

I wonder if I'm telling her too much, but I do have to trust that she's keeping my friends safe and that she will do as she promised.

Jasmine says, "Let's get going. Make sure the prisoners can't escape."

We start walking, her guards surrounding the dwarf soldiers. They look subdued and they all have their hands tied behind their backs. I'm surprised none are hurt. That they came out of the explosion unscathed is noteworthy.

I decide to test the power without the collar. I concentrate on a patch of road on the other side of the wide boulevard. The streets are deserted so I don't have to worry about hurting anyone. I send a small amount of power at the road, and it erupts like the last explosions did. There is a large crater, and pieces of the road along with the underlying gravel go spraying twenty meters into the sky.

I concentrate again, this time trying harder to send just a small amount of power. It erupts and causes a crater just as large as the first, but I think, and maybe it's just hopeful thinking, that the crater is a little smaller.

It seems my power has grown and gotten out of control despite the white gold. Or maybe the new collar has given me power that stays with me along with a lack of control. There must be some way for me to reign it in. I will keep trying.

We get back to Jasmine's house and the prisoners are taken underground to the dungeon. I wonder if dungeons might be a common feature of a dwarf's home. More likely just for those in charge.

Jasmine gets busy assembling her army. I find a quiet spot where no one will get hurt and try again and again to lessen the impact of my magic. Each time I leave a giant crater no matter how small the amount of energy I think I'm sending. The frustration in me is probably making things worse, so I stop and wander back to where everyone is getting ready.

With her army assembled, Jasmine leads them out onto the street, and we head to the north gate. I am surprised to see a few ogres with the dwarf army. They don't have collars, so they must be here of their own choosing.

I ask Jasmine, "How did you persuade those ogres to help you?"

Jasmine says, "They have always been loyal to the council. They are all born and raised here in the city. They are as much a part of us as any dwarf is."

I mark this information under strange and complicated. How can people serve the very ones who enslave their people?

There is more activity on the streets now. Some things are returning to normal. The market is not far, and the sounds of people mingling and buying can be heard. The streets are not as clean as they should be, and that will probably get worse before it gets better.

Anyone who sees us coming soon disappears. Dwarf or other, no one is keen to be too close to an army. We reach the north gates, where many dwarf soldiers guard it. Jasmine looks at me. "Time to keep your side of the bargain, Hawk."

The gate is fifty meters off yet, and I see a lot of dwarves and ogres lined up behind it. I don't sense any collars, so either the ogres are there because they want to be, or the collars are white gold. I call out to them, "I am of the Light. I am going to blow down your gate. Please stand back, as I don't want anyone to get hurt."

The guards look at each other, but no one moves.

I decide maybe I need to talk louder. I move a little closer and try again. "I am a powerful mage and I'm going to blow up your gate. I have no wish to harm anyone, so please stand back from the gate."

Someone calls out, "We are waiting for King Ruuc. He is on his way. Please don't do anything just yet."

Jasmine says, "I guess Ruuc wants to talk. I imagine he thinks he can keep his power. Just blow the gate down, Hawk. Knock it down, and we'll get this all over with."

I ask her, "Why wouldn't you at least want to hear what the king has to say?"

Jasmine replies, "Because he's deceitful. I'm sure this is just some kind of trick. He'll lure us in for a parley and take us all hostage or worse, kill us."

I shake my head. Something isn't right about all this. Jasmine's words sound reasonable, but I can't imagine Ruuc doing something quite that nasty. He seemed reasonable to me, for a dwarf anyway.

"What are you not telling me, Jasmine?"

"Nothing, Hawk. I'm not hiding anything from you. Ruuc will most likely take us all hostage or kill us if he gets the chance. He's desperate to hold on to his power."

Just then, the gates open and a contingent of dwarves and ogres march through holding pikes towards us.

Jasmine says, "Charge them! Take the gate!"

Jasmine's army starts to surge forward. I can't help but think that something is wrong. She seemed nervous as soon as Ruuc's name was mentioned and that he was coming. Why would Jasmine be afraid of talking to Ruuc? Was there some secret he knew that she didn't want aired? Maybe something that would make her people turn against her? There is a tickling in my brain that just maybe this has something to do with me.

As the soldiers march towards each other, I aim power and blow a hole in the road between them. Pieces of rock and dust blow far up into the air. Both armies stop, covered by a dust cloud. I walk forward.

Jasmine says, "Hawk, don't do that. Stop. Ruuc will capture you."

"Maybe, but I think he knows something you don't want me to know."

Jasmine says, "Kill him! Kill the human mage! He's going to betray us!"

I turn and face her and her soldiers. "Everyone stop. I don't want to hurt any of you. I've had enough pain and death for one life already. But if you try to stop me, I will kill you. I don't know if any of you were there when Wuruch died, but I'm sure you've heard of it. Everyone stay where you are."

When I'm sure none of them are going to march on me, I turn back to Ruuc's soldiers. The dust is settling now, and I can see figures beyond. Peering through the thinning cloud, I see a couple trolls and a smallish figure, a short squat one with a crown on his head. I walk towards them. One of the trolls scratches her left shoulder.

It can't be, can it? Jasmine was lying to me about where my friends were?

I hear Sam bark and then I know. I start running to them.

Chapter Twenty

Power's Resolution

I hug Sam and laugh as he licks my entire face. I've never been so glad to be slobbered on. I stand up and keep my hand on his head. "Chortnel, Grain, Flavor, Truut, and Dolain. I'm glad you all are alive. I was told you were put on a boat for the next quadrant. Where are the rest of the former slaves?"

An ogre comes forward. "We are taking over the palace."

I notice Flavor has a bandage around her middle. I say, "I'm glad you survived that battle. Will you be okay?"

Flavor says, "It's only a flesh wound, I'll be fine."

Ruuc speaks up, "The former slaves are trying to take over the palace, but they will fail. My guards are fighting them now as we speak."

I am not sure what to do. Between Ruuc, Jasmine, and the former slaves, anything might happen. All I want is to get Sam and I on a boat headed for the next quadrant. I look at Dolain. "Do you speak for the former slaves?"

Dolain nods. "They listen to me yes."

I look at Ruuc and Jasmine and say, "Maybe we can find a quiet place for the three of you to work this out while I and my friends go to the docks and leave you all to your fighting and power grab stuff."

Ruuc and Jasmine both protest, looking at each other and gritting their teeth. I say, "I'm not staying to help either of you, or you." I look in Dolain's direction. "I just don't care who runs things here as long as there are no more slaves. Ruuc, can you give me some dwarf sailors?"

Ruuc says, "Let's go inside and we can talk. Jasmine, you can bring five of your soldiers with you? The rest will need to wait out here."

Jasmine picks five of her soldiers, then we all walk into the palace. The gates are closed behind us. We walk down a wide corridor. On either side are tapestries showing various battle scenes and statues depicting dwarves. I have trouble telling them apart, but I suppose the statues aren't all of the same person.

We near the end of the wide corridor when a contingent of armed ogres, trolls, and elves appears in front of us. I look behind and the way back to the gates is blocked by another contingent.

Ruuc wastes no time. He commands his troops to charge, forward and to the rear. There is fighting, but I can do nothing about it without risking damage or hurting someone. The fighting is too close, and any attempt at throwing power is going to cause damage to the corridor and to anyone near the explosion. All I can do is watch while Ruuc's soldiers battle it out with the former slaves.

An ogre grabs a pike from one of the soldiers and starts swinging it. He goes down when someone throws a knife, piercing the large ogre in the heart. Several mages stand in the middle of weapon-wielding soldiers, but they are of no use. I can't see or feel even one collar among the fighters. The rear fighting is stopped when the former slaves run off. The ones in front keep fighting, but now the king's soldiers are reinforced with the contingent that had been fighting behind them.

Soon, the fighting is over. A few of the former slaves are captured and the rest have run off. Dolain remains with us. I wonder why he didn't run off with the others. Ruuc issues some commands, then the former slaves along with Jasmine and her followers are led off.

Jasmine protests. "My people will attack if I don't show up in a few hours. You'd be better off listening to me, Ruuc. We can still work this out."

Ruuc shakes his head and looks at me. "I don't trust her."

I say, "She lied to me. She told me Sam and my friends were on a boat bound for the next quadrant and if I didn't do what she asked, she would send a boat of soldiers after them to kill them."

Chortnel says, "The king has been taking care of us, Hawk. No barred cells, and we have rooms of our own."

Grain adds, "Ya, but there are guards outside the rooms."

Ruuc says, "I had to know you'd all be safe." He starts walking. "Come, let's talk about your future, Hawk."

I say, "My future is a boat bound for the next quadrant. All I need from you is a pilot and crew to take me there. I've given you enough to deserve that at least."

Ruuc says, "But you could be very rich and powerful here, Hawk. Stay and be my wizard, and together we can rule the world."

"I have no desire to rule the world. I just want to get on with this quest. If it's as important as people say it is, then you need to let me go. If you don't, your entire kingdom, not to mention the entire world, is in danger."

Ruuc says, "If what they say is true. But seriously, you think you were meant to save the entire world, Hawk?" He laughs, then shakes his head. "You're big compared to us dwarves, but you are young and small for a human, yes?"

I shrug. "I'm still growing. I know what I'm doing."

Ruuc says, "But do you? Really? If you stay and work with me, you can have anything you want. You help me, and I will make you rich."

I say, "I just want to see the next quadrant and figure out these visions I get when I'm out under the clouds."

Ruuc says, "Stay long enough for the three sides to come to an agreement. That's all I'll ask. You and your friends can rest for a day, can't you?"

I shake my head. I'm so done with this whole place, all the dwarves and the fighting. "I don't know why I'd want that." I stop and look at the king. "I understand, you're the king and you are used to getting your way. You say what gets done and not done. But I'm not a part of this world of yours, I was forced into it, and now it's time I left it and got on with things." I look at the dwarf guards around me. "Do any of you know how to row and maybe pilot a boat?"

They don't answer me. They don't even look like they heard me. Ruuc sighs. "I understand your impatience. I'm sure I would feel the same in your place, but if you could just stay long enough to let Jasmine and the former slaves see that you are on my side, they will be forced to deal with me."

I guess I'd kept a lot of anger inside me. I don't know what else could explain what I did just then. I look down a corridor that is deserted and blow it up. I just felt the power in me, focused it on a spot in the corridor far enough away so no one would get hurt, and I sent. The explosion rocks the floor we stand on. Several people are startled, and many land on their backsides. A cloud of smoke and dust covers the hole I've made.

I do my best not to look guilty or sheepish. The Light take me, it felt good to do that, like letting go all the anger and frustration that had been building up in me. I hadn't tried to contain the energy; I'd just focused and let go.

I look at King Ruuc. "I want a few sailors to come with me to the dock, find a boat, and get going." I say it quietly, letting the damage I'd done speak for me.

Ruuc looks at what had been done to his palace. I think he might be contemplating trying to kill me, but he says. "I don't have any sailors at hand among these guards, but come with me, I promise I will send for a half dozen and make sure there's a boat waiting for you at the docks."

I say, "Okay, but if you don't, there will be more of these craters."

Ruuc nods. "I understand, please just give me a few more minutes." He leads us down the corridor, and I can see daylight at the end of it. I glance over at my friends. Grain and Flavor seem unperturbed, but the rest are eyeing me carefully, like I might just decide to explode and kill everyone within reach.

We enter a large area with trees, flowers, and a small pond in the center. The king calls for servants and gives them instructions to set up a large table for a meeting. He turns to another servant and tells them to go find six sailors who can make the trip now to the next quadrant.

He turns to me. "I'm going to have Jasmine and that elf Dolain brought up here to talk. You can say your goodbyes and be off with a crew to take you to the next quadrant. Fair enough?"

"You want them to see me with you, giving me what I want."

Ruuc shrugs. "It might be enough to give me an edge if they think I've given you a favor. I'm going to get ready for this meeting and find you a few sailors, I'll return soon." He walks off with his contingent of guards.

Chortnel comes to me, scratching her shoulder. I ask, "Does your baby have a name yet?"

Chortnel shakes her head. "It would be against our traditions to name a child before it is separated from its mother."

I say, "But you must have something in mind, don't you?"

Chortnel grimaces, which sort of looks the same as her smile, but I'm starting to recognize the differences in her facial expressions. She says, "We don't talk of names until the separation. But I want to talk to you about your power. It's become very impressive. Do you even need a source to draw the power from?"

"I don't seem to now."

Chortnel says, "We must find a way for you to control it."

I nod. "That is a priority. Do you think Ruuc will keep his word and let us go?"

"I don't think you give him much choice. Either he lets you go, or you go on wreaking havoc on his palace."

Grain and Flavor come to join us. Grain says, "How's your head, Hawk? Have you had any more headaches or blackouts?"

I say, "None since the last time I saw you. I feel fine, but this power I have keeps growing and I'm losing any ability to control it."

Ruuc comes back, and soon six dwarves are coming over to where we stand. At the same time, Jasmine and Dolain are led to the table that is now set up with food and drink. Ruuc says, "Would you care for something to eat and drink before you leave, Hawk?"

I look at my companions. Grain says, "We are all fine. I think Hawk just wants to get going."

Ruuc nods. "Will you say goodbye to Jasmine and Dolain, Hawk?"

"Yes, okay." I walk to the table. "Jasmine, Dolain, I wish you both well in talks. I hope that you all can resolve your differences and return the city to normalcy."

Jasmine says, "Thank you, Hawk. I apologize for my deception, and I hope you find what it is you search for."

Dolain says, "I wish you well my friend, and I want to thank you for giving us our lives back. We will never forget you. I hope at some point in the future we will meet again."

I walk to where Ruuc is standing. I tell him, "I hope Fuutenhold will be okay. Thank you for the sailors, Ruuc, and I wish you the best of luck."

Ruuc comes and grabs my arm. "May your journey save us all, Hawk Archer. I wish you well."

I turn to the gate. "Okay, let's get going."

We walk out of the gate and head for the docks. There is some movement, but the streets are still partially filled with garbage and offal. It's not the clean and vibrant city that I saw when I first came, but it is a free city at least. For now, anyway.

We get to the docks without incident and there is a large boat waiting for us. We all board and no one speaks as the sailors dip oars and start to row toward the tunnel. I watch the city slowly disappear behind us as we finally start the next part of the journey.

Chapter Twenty-One

A Pirate Encounter

I sit against the bow, feet outstretched, Sam's head resting on my thigh as I stroke his fur. It feels good to be back with him. I vow I won't let anyone or anything separate us again. The rhythm of the oars slicing into and coming out of the water is soothing.

Chortnel says, "When we get to the docks, we will be in the second quadrant. I hope that means you won't get the vision, Hawk, but we should try to prepare if you do."

My brain refuses to think. I just want to drift off into sleep. We should be at the docks in a couple hours. "Let me rest, Chortnel, I've had enough of thinking and doing. I just want to sleep a bit."

Chortnel says, "But we must have a plan. If the vision takes you, you could die. We must think of a way to pull you out and back into this corridor if it takes you."

I sigh. She's right, I suppose.

Grain says, "I could keep your head healing while we move to the docks. It might provide protection."

I say, "If the vision does take me, what can I do? Come back into the waterway and hide? I can't stay away forever." I turn to Grain. "I think you are my best hope if I do get the vision."

Then I look at Chortnel. "I don't know what else I can do. If I black out, try to get the dwarves to turn around, I guess."

The steady rowing has my eyelids getting heavy, and I close them, thinking I'll just rest a bit. But I come back from sleep with a start. I look around me, but there's not much to see. Chortnel and Grain are sleeping. The tunnel is dark ahead, and behind, the covered torches show only a little ways in front of us.

Then a soft glow appears in front of me and the whisper in my head is less powerful and the words have changed. It says, "Find her," and I see a girl about my age. She has long, black hair and almond shaped eyes. Her skin color is lighter than mine, but not as light as Wexley's was.

I get the feeling she must be a wizard like me. I wonder how the Light I'm supposed to find her, but at least the vision isn't killing me. I nudge Chortnel. "Chortnel, wake up, I've had a vision."

Chortnel shakes her head, scratches the shoulder her baby is attached to, and moans. "A what?"

"A vision. I just had a vision about a girl I'm supposed to find, and we are getting to the end of the tunnel. I can see light now."

Chortnel rubs her eyes and sits up to look, but just then there is a crash, and we are all thrown forward as the boat comes to a stop. There are two of the dwarf boats, one on either side of us. They have come in so close that they have pushed the oars up against the hull, making them useless.

I stand up and feel for the power. It's there, but I won't use it. There is too much chance of something going wrong. I look into the boat next to my side and see a half dozen people, two humans, a troll, an ogre, and two elves in the group.

On the other side, a large black man and five other humans are staring us down.

The black man says, "Greetings travelers, you have been captured by none other than Mr. Sparks. I will need you to give up anything you have of value and move to the front of the boat." As he says this, the people with him reveal bows nocked with an arrow each.

"Now, let's keep things civilized so my friends here don't have to put holes in any of you. Go along now, to the bow with you all."

The only people who aren't in the bow are the rowers. Six dwarves move up to the front of the boat with us.

"Wonderful! You've all been excellent guests so far. Now if you will all keep your hands where we can see them, we'll get this over with very soon."

The two humans, along with the ogre, troll, and elves, board us from that side of the boat. They are carrying lengths of rope. Two of the men lash our boat to theirs. The others begin tying us up, our hands behind our backs.

Mr. Sparks says, "Just a precaution, folks, no need to worry, we'll be done here very soon."

Once everyone is tied up, their belongings and pockets are searched. The loot is piled together in the middle while the troll and two elves go through the rest of the boat searching. When they are done, Mr. Sparks looks over what they've taken. A few food items, a small pile of jewels and gold coins.

Mr. Sparks says, "Right then, not a very wealthy lot, are you?"

Chortnel speaks up, "We're mostly former slaves. We don't have very much, and we just want to get to the next quadrant."

Mr. Sparks comes over to Chortnel, noticing she is scratching her shoulder and turns her. He makes a strange sound, sort of like an owl, I think. He places a finger under the baby's chin. The baby growls and tries to bite his finger.

Mr. Sparks says, "Tsk, your young trolls are always so aggressive. When will she be born, do you think?"

Chortnel says, "Soon, a few weeks."

Mr. Sparks nods and turns to the dwarves. "Well my friends, we will say our goodbyes to you." He nods to the ogres, who have moved themselves so each one stands behind a dwarf. At Mr. Spark's nod, they all pull out knives, and while I think they are about to kill our dwarf sailors, instead they cut the ropes binding their arms. Then each ogre picks up a dwarf and throws them over the bow into the water.

Mr. Sparks waves at them and says, "Safe trip into port! You've got maybe a twenty-minute swim if you are determined." He laughs and turns to us. "My friends, you will accompany me and my mates here to our town. You will be our guests while you decide your own fates."

I ask him, "What do you mean, decide our own fates?"

Mr. Sparks smiles at me. There is something not right with his eyes; they sort of glitter. His smile doesn't make me feel welcome; it makes me feel like I'm facing a grinning werewolf. He says, "You will get to choose. Either stay with us and become part of my family, or you can be sold into slavery."

Chortnel says, "Mr. Sparks, this is Hawk Archer." She points at me. "Do you know that name?"

Mr. Sparks strokes his chin and looks up like he's looking at the clouds of the night, but there's nothing there, just darkness and the tunnel ceiling. He looks back at Chortnel. "There's a rumor I think about your Mr. Archer. Some sort of wizard, is he?" He grins at me. "You going to cause me problems, young man?"

I am not quick with a reply. I'd like very much to cause this man problems, but using my power is out of the question. I say, "No, no problem, but I have been given a quest by the Light and I keep having visions. They won't go away unless I do what the Light wants me to."

Mr. Sparks looks at me curiously. "Well, let's get under way and we can talk about your visions." He nods to his compatriots, and they return to their boats. They each maneuver in front of our boat and then lines are brought out and tied to pins in the railings.

Mr. Sparks says, "We will tow you to our little town, and we can talk more there, but tell me, Mr. Archer, about your visions."

The boats start moving, the light coming from the end of the tunnel grows stronger, and soon we are out of the tunnel and into a large body of water, much larger than any lake I've ever seen. Straight ahead, the water stretches far into the distance, with no land in sight.

To the right of us, I hear splashing and look over to see the dwarves swimming. They are not far from the beach as we pass them. Off in the distance that way, I see docks and the familiar sight of a town. There's a town square with a talking stand in the middle, covered with a wooden roof held up by white pillars.

It recedes from us as our captors row parallel to the rocks on our left. We are leaving the cave entrance, but I can't see anything but rock walls there, not like the wall I found, but more like the mountain home of the dwarves.

I tell Mr. Sparks about my visions and how they started.

"I'm from a small town in the quadrant to the west, where we came from. The day for the 100,000 celebration, I started having visions of a tunnel that I found in the dome. A voice kept whispering 'come' to me in my head. The visions got stronger and stronger, until just before

Chortnel and I were sold as slaves to the dwarves, the vision was so powerful it knocked me senseless. I haven't had any since going under the dwarves' mountain to their city, Fuutenhold."

I'm not going to tell him about the new vision. This Mr. Sparks doesn't seem quite right. He's polite enough, but I sense a deep mean streak in him. I think I will just keep the new vision to myself.

Mr. Sparks says, "We were all slaves once."

Chortnel asks, "How did you get away?"

Mr. Sparks smiles. "Violence, my pregnant troll, we resorted to violence. What is your name?"

"I'm Chortnel."

Mr. Sparks looks at my other companions in turn.

"I'm Flavor."

"I'm Grain."

Mr. Sparks bends down to pat Sam on the head, but he growls and bares his teeth. Mr. Sparks laughs and stands straight. "Well, my newfound friends, we will show you our town and let you eat and rest for a day. Tomorrow you will make your decision to stay with us or..." He shrugs and smiles. "Become slaves again," he finishes.

I ask him, "You would sell us into slavery even though you were once a slave?"

Mr. Sparks shrugs. "I don't see why not. I'm always on the lookout for a few gold pieces. But if you stay with us, and become part of my family, I'll make you a deal. You can work for me for a year and earn enough to buy your freedom, and I won't sell you into slavery."

It doesn't sound like much of an option to me, but I don't say anything just yet. The boats are turning in toward the rocks now and it looks like they are going to tow us right into them. As we pass a few gray boulders, I notice there's a channel they are following. I don't see it until we are being towed into it by the two boats in front of us.

The channel leads through the rocks, and twists left and then right. Above us, not visible from the lake, are several elves with bows. They stare down at us, then wave to Mr. Sparks.

He waves back and says, "We are a close family. We take care of each other. Those boys and girls up there make sure no one can sneak up on us. The only way in or out of our town is this channel. Of course..." He smiles and winks at the three of us. "They make sure no one leaves without permission either."

The boats are coming out from the rocks now. I can see docks on the left as the channel widens out into a small bay. The dock we head for has four ogres waiting for us. I notice Flavor looking at them intently. When we are at the dock, the rowers jump out of the left boat and secure it. One of the elves jumps into our boat. Flavor stands up as one of the ogres on the dock tosses a rope to the elf.

Flavor says, "It's good to see you, Gar, Loam, Salt, and Rock."

One of the ogres breaks out in what I think is a grin. "Boss, good to see you too."

Chapter Twenty-Two

A New Arrival

Flavor's garden pulls our boat close to the dock. The boat is lashed at the bow and stern to thick poles designed for such things. There are large round cloth balls set between dock and boat to keep them from grinding on each other. A plank, about a meter wide, is set between dock and boat. The ogres come aboard and lead us off.

Flavor asks, "Salt, where is Loma?"

Salt says, "Loma went home. Mr. Sparks said he'd let one of us go if the rest of us stayed and work for him."

Flavor asks, "Can you take these ropes off us? We aren't going anywhere." Salt glances at Mr. Sparks, who shakes his head.

"Sorry Flavor. Boss say no."

I ask Mr. Sparks, "What are you going to do with us?"

He replies, "We will take you to the guest house, let you get rested, and then we'll talk in the morning." His voice is cheery, and he smiles way too much for my comfort.

We are led to a long house made of logs. The roof is sloped and seems to be made of some kind of sod. There are plants and grass growing out of it.

Mr. Spark says, "Go inside now, and food and drink will be along in no time. Get your rest my friends, as tomorrow will be time for decision making." He bows to us, then laughs and takes off.

The house is lit from windows at the four corners, two each on the long side of the place, one on each end. There are beds at one end and a table with several sturdy chairs on the other. There are sconces all along the walls. Some have torches in them, but none are lit at the moment. The ogre called Salt cuts our bonds one by one.

"Go sit at the table for now," he tells Grain when her ropes are off. He does the same for Chortnel and then me. He cuts Flavor's ropes last. "Someone will bring you a meal soon. We'll be back in the morning for you." He walks out, shuts the door, and there's a sound of a large bar sliding into place. The sound makes me think of the jail back home.

The table and chairs are well constructed. Grain runs her hands over a chair, and then a table. "Elven craft. Well made and sturdy." She sits down. "What do we do now?"

I take a seat and look around. I could blow a hole in one of the walls, but what then?

I say, "I think we just have to wait until morning."

Chortnel sits next to me, scratching her shoulder and now her side where the baby is still attached. "I don't think we are getting out of here using that channel we came in on. Maybe there's another way out?"

Flavor sits. "I think my garden will help us."

I shake my head. "It looks to me like they answer to Sparks now."

Flavor gets a look on her face. I haven't seen it before. Then I see a tear on her cheek running down and then around her right tusk.

"Flavor, are you alright? Why are you crying?"

She sniffles, and a glob of greenish goo comes out of her nose. She wipes it away absently and looks at me. "A garden is for life. Everything changed when we were dwarven slaves, but now they change more. My garden doesn't belong to me." She chokes on a sob.

Grain moves next to her and pats her massive shoulder. "It's okay, they probably have to pretend to like Sparks. I bet they are somewhere figuring out just how to free you even as we talk about it."

Flavor sniffles. "You really think so?"

Grain says, "Of course I do. Your garden wouldn't just change and turn on you. You'll see, they will wait for the right moment and then free us."

I say, "I hope so." Then a vision takes me again. 'Find her.' Grain and Flavor look like they are underwater, I see their lips move but I can't hear what they are saying. I have a vague memory of when I was a child. I was dropped in the pond and submerged in water. I look up and see Ma talking to my Da. She's angry with him and he's trying to reason with her. There's a sound in my ears, the water filling them, I suppose. Then Ma reaches into the water and pulls me out. My ears clear, then I hear them fighting about Da pushing me in the water.

I can see Flavor and Grain, and over to one side Chortnel sits and watches them. Then my vision clears and the image of the girl I saw before comes swimming in front of my eyes. She's smiling and twirling her fingers.

Then everything clears back to normal, and I hear Chortnel say, "Hawk, you alright?" She comes over and sits by me, putting a hand on my shoulder. "You just had a vision, didn't you?"

Now Grain and Flavor stop talking, Grain gets up and comes next to me. She puts hands on either side of my head and says, "Look at me." I blink and look into her strange eyes that look like a cat's. She blinks and asks me, "Are you okay? Does your head hurt?"

I say, "No, I'm fine, but the vision is different now. I see the face of a girl and the voice says to find her."

Chortnel asks, "Did the vision tell you where to look?"

I think about that, about the first vision. Was there a place I saw? It's fuzzy now except for the face of the girl. I think I will always remember that face, calm but with eyes that flash at me. I imagine those eyes burning holes in anyone she might be angry with. Maybe she had the power too? Maybe she can teach me how to control it.

I say, "I'm not sure. Mostly I just see her face and I know, I think anyway, that she has power like I do. I think she and I are meant for the same quest."

Chortnel says, "Maybe you should try and practice, Hawk. See if you can learn to control this fire."

I think about the huge lake. It would be a good place to practice control. The water would absorb any heat or damage I might generate.

I say, "If we get the chance."

The door is unbarred and opened. Several people come in. Three are carrying plates and metal goblets. They are humans, two women and a man. They set the food and drink on the table and leave.

The others are an elf, a troll, and three of Flavor's ogres. There is one more, a type of person I've never seen before. It is short and covered in dark fur. There are white stripes extending down its back, and it stands about the same height as an ordinary dwarf. The voice is vaguely feminine.

"I am Drafa, Mistress of this village, Seacove. I want you to know you will be as comfortable as I can make you. Is there anything you wish?"

I say, "My freedom."

She smiles at me. Her white teeth are pointed and gleaming. That is not a mouth I want to meet on a dark night. "Sparks will discuss with you your options in the morning."

I say, "Why do you let Sparks keep captives?"

Drafa looks at me. "Why should I care what Sparks does? He brings us prosperity, and in return I give him a place, a home to live in."

She leaves, and the troll and elf follow her. The three ogres remain, standing there and looking awkward. I think they are feeling guilty.

Flavor doesn't say a word, she just looks towards the door, sadness coating her face like a drizzling rain. Finally, one ogre speaks. "We ask Sparks to release you."

Flavor slowly turns her head and stares at the one who spoke. "What did he say?"

"He say he talk with you in the morning." He pulls out three cubes with dots on them and sets them on the table. "I leave you the games. So the night go faster."

As they reach the door, Flavor says, "Salt, you stay?"

The ogres all stop and turn to her. Salt says, "We play games?"

Flavor says, "Make the night go faster."

The ogres all huff through their noses. I don't know what that means but they all sit at a table and start talking in ogreish and taking turns picking up the cubes and tossing them on the table.

I ask Chortnel, "What are they doing?"

Chortnel tells me, "They are being friends again, Hawk." She says this like it's the most obvious thing in the world.

I say, "I see that, but why? Her garden betrayed her, took her captive, but now they are all best buddies?"

Chortnel looks at me and says, "I think humans hold grudges to be too important. They were friends and it's much better to be friends now, isn't it?"

I shake my head and try to imagine playing a game with Preacher and Stiggs. But that isn't the same thing, I guess. Preacher and Stiggs were never my friends and they had tried to kill me.

Dahlia was sort of a friend, I think. I look at Sam, who is sitting in the corner, head on his paws, eyes drooping. He's about to go to sleep. Sam is the only real good friend I've had until I met Chortnel and Grain. I wonder if it's odd that I had to leave home in order to find friends.

Chortnel gasps, and I come out of my thoughts to see she is holding her shoulder. Grain stans and goes to her, placing her hands on Chortnel's back. I move closer. "What's wrong, Chortnel?"

"Baby is coming," she says, pain in her voice.

I ask, "What can I do to help?"

Chortnel relaxes a little as Grain soothes her with the elven magic. She says, "I need water to wash the baby with. Get what you can."

I move over to where the ogres are playing and say, "Chortnel's baby is coming, and she needs water. Can you go get us a couple buckets of it?"

The one called Salt stands and looks at Chortnel. "Baby comes now? I don't think that good idea."

I say, "I don't think she has a choice. The baby wants to be born and that's it. Can you help?"

Chortnel calls out, "And some food. She'll be hungry. Live fish is best, but anything alive will do."

I remember the werewolves and the shaggy beast. Chortnel tore into it with as much gusto as the wolves had. I look at Sam. Maybe I should stay close to him.

Salt grinds his teeth and makes a low rumbling noise. He leaves the house. The rest of us move to surround Chortnel and Grain. Chortnel is breathing hard, her eyes closed. I can't really see what's going on with the baby as the ogres all crowd me out.

When I move to the side, I can see a little arm and leg flailing.

One of the ogres says, "She is strong and healthy. She will make fine troll."

There's a sound then, a sort of screeching noise. I look at Chortnel, but she's not making it. The arm and leg are pressed against Chortnel's side, trying to push away. Chortnel's eyes are closed, her mouth set in firm lines she looks like she is trying to lift a large weight. There is quiet strain on her face. Another screech, and it sounds like something ripping. I see blood dripping down Chortnel's side.

"Are you okay, Chortnel? Is something wrong?"

Flavor says, "Nothing wrong, baby is coming."

Salt returns with two buckets of water. "I ask Drafa to bring us fresh fish."

Flavor grabs a tablecloth and dips it in the water. She begins washing the baby, then pulls her hand back in surprise.

"Ow, she has sharp teeth, watch out."

I hear another screech and the baby pulls away some more. Grain is holding Chortnel's head. Chortnel is straining to not move. The ogres look at the baby coming out with fascination on their faces. There's another ripping sound, then the little arm and leg move a bit further away from Chortnel's back. I'm glad I'm not able to stand with the ogres and watch all this. I'd probably get sick.

Flavor wipes the tablecloth over Chortnel's back, then dips it in the bucket of water and wrings it out.

There is a sucking noise, a screech, and Chortnel wails in pain. The baby troll plops out of its mother and falls to the floor. It looks at us and hisses. It grabs on to Grain and bites her. Grain screams and smacks the baby away from her. The baby falls to the floor again, but now there's blood on her lips. She looks around. I move slowly back to where Sam is lying, eyes closed. I have no idea how he can still be asleep, but I put myself between him and the baby troll. She blinks at me, then looks at Sam and comes at us fast. I'm surprised at how fast the little thing is. By the Light, I'm surprised at its nasty temper. Chortnel might try to seem bad and threatening, but really no troll I've met has ever acted like this.

    The baby moves quick. She wants to eat my best friend.

Chapter Twenty-Three

A Pirate's Life

The baby troll is about half the size of Sam. She's moving fast and she looks hungry. As she gets close, I reach out to grab her before she can bite into my dog, but I miss.

From behind me Sam wakes up with a startled yelp and starts letting the entire world know about his pain. I reach for the baby, who is now latched onto Sam's backside, trying to tear out a chunk of dog meat. I grab her arms and pull. Sam howls even louder now. The baby has her teeth sunk into Sam's butt and won't let go.

The door opens and Drafa comes in with two buckets. I see tails flopping around in both of them. She looks at Sam in alarm and rushes over. I try to pull the baby troll off Sam as Drafa sets the buckets down, pulls out a fish, and slaps it across baby's face. The baby blinks but doesn't let go. She sniffs the air and Drafa slaps the fish against her cheek again.

Baby growls and finally lets go of Sam. She looks at me and hisses. I still have her by her arms and I think it's a good idea to keep on holding her.

I tell Drafa, "Put a fish in her mouth."

Drafa says, "You have to let go. She will go to the fish. Trolls prefer water flesh over land flesh any day."

I look toward Chortnel for advice, but she's hunched over, eyes closed and panting. Grain is watching Sam and the baby while using her healing power to help Chortnel. She bites her lip, and I think she wants to be in both places to help Sam and Chortnel. But of course, that isn't possible.

I decide to trust Drafa. Poor Sam is whining and licking the wound. I need to help him as best I can. I let go of the baby's arms and she pounces on the fish. Drafa drops another one a little closer to Chortnel, leading the baby back to her mother.

Baby grabs the flopping fish and bites deep into its side, then wrenches out a hunk of pink flesh. The fish is nearly the same size as she is, but the little troll is so hungry it devours the first fish in three bites. She swallows what's left, then looks around for her next victim before Drafa drops another fish. It flops on the ground a few steps towards Chortnel. The baby pounces again, devouring that fish in a few bites.

Drafa takes a few steps away from Sam and me and drops another wriggling fish. The baby pounces yet again.

I see that Drafa has control of the situation and I turn to Sam, touching his fur gently. He's bleeding, but it's not gushing out, thank the Light. I pet his head as Sam licks away at the wound. I look toward Grain, who looks back at me, concern on her face.

She says, "I'll be there to help in a moment, Hawk."

Chortnel opens her eyes to see her daughter grabbing a fish that flops at Chortnel's feet. Drafa sets the bucket down by Chortnel and hands her a fish. She pats Mama troll on her right shoulder, the one still intact.

She asks Chortnel, "Is this your first baby?"

Chortnel shakes her head. "It's been many years but no, she is not my first."

Drafa nods, "Well, she'll calm down now that her belly is full, I think."

Chortnel looks grateful. "Thank you, Drafa. How do you know so much about troll babies?"

Drafa grins, her sharp teeth gleaming. "You live long enough, you see most everything."

Chortnel smiles weakly. The baby hops on Chortnel's lap and offers her mother a still wriggling fish.

Chortnel strokes the baby's head. "Thank you dear. That's kind of you to offer your mother food." Chortnel takes it and bites off the head. Baby relaxes a little, then cuddles into her mother's lap and closes her eyes. A large burp comes from the little one's mouth, then there is the sound of soft snoring.

Grain pats Chortnel gently and moves over to me and Sam. She touches the wound lightly, and Sam wags his tail and whines.

Grain said, "She took quite a bite out of him."

I said, "Yeah, I'll have to remember to keep Sam away from birthing trolls in the future. Do you think you can heal it?"

Grain places her hands on either side. "There will be a scar, I'm afraid, but I'll close the wound and keep it from festering." Her hands glow softly, and I realize the light is fading. Chortnel picks up her baby and moves to the area where the beds are. She chooses a bed and cuddles the baby in her arms. Soon there are sounds of two trolls snoring.

I look back at Sam's hind end. The wound is closed and dry. It is now a patch of hairless skin but at least looks far less painful.

I said, "Thank you, Grain. Sam and I are lucky you are with us."

She smiles and stands. "I'm off to bed now. Are you going to bed or staying here?"

I eye the bed holding Chortnel. "I think Sam and I will be just fine here. At least for tonight." Sam already has his head on his paws and is close to resuming his rudely interrupted sleep.

"Good night, Hawk Archer. See you in the morning." Grain goes to the beds. The ogres talk in low tones. The soft rattle of their gaming cubes is soothing. I put my head on Sam's back and turn on my side. I close my eyes and sleep.

I wake up to the clanging of pots together. I open my eyes and turn towards the din. I can see a couple ogres and Mr. Sparks with cooking vessels, making a racket. Sparks has his overly bright smile. His eyes shine with relish.

"Wake up, me lads and lasses! The clouds give us light, and we must not waste the gift. On your feet now!"

Sam starts awake and stands up, and my head bumps on the floor. I rub the sore spot as I sit up and yawn.

I say, "What is all this noise for? Is it really necessary?"

Mr. Sparks comes over near me, banging his pots. "Today is your first day as a pirate, lad. It's a thing to celebrate and make noise over." He laughs and bangs his pots as he moves to the room with the beds.

I yawn again and stand. On the table are steaming bowls. A mug stands next to each bowl and steam rises from them as well. I go over and sit down in front of a bowl. I pick it up and smell it. There is a tangy sweet smell. I pick up the wooden spoon next the bowl and take a bite. It's warm and creamy in my mouth, and the tangy taste is very good.

Sam sits next to me, sniffing the air. I don't see any meat, but I notice there are two buckets at the end of the table with tails sticking up out of them. Fresh fish, the same as what Drafa brought to Chortnel.

I pull one of the fish out. It's fat, sleek, and about 30 centimeters long. I give it to Sam, who sniffs it briefly then takes it in his mouth and moves to the wall to lie down and enjoy his breakfast.

Chortnel comes in holding her baby. She also sees the buckets of fish and takes one to the other side of the table, sitting opposite me.

Chortnel says, "Hawk, I want to apologize for the baby's behavior last night. I hope that Sam is okay." She sets the baby next to her and gives her a fish. Then Chortnel grabs one, and mother and daughter both take a bite.

I say, "Grain healed him, and he's fine. How are you? It looked like having a baby is very painful the way trolls do it."

Chortnel grins. "You haven't seen the way humans do it, have you?"

I shake my head. "In our village, women having babies are kept in a house, and only other women are allowed inside."

Mr. Sparks joins us, along with Grain and Flavor. Flavor's ogre friends didn't stay the night. Only the two that came with Mr. Sparks are here.

They all sit down and pick up a bowl. Mr. Sparks inhales deeply. "I love the smell of oranges." He picks up a spoon and puts a heaping portion of the gruel in his mouth.

I make short work of breakfast and end with a polite burp. Mr. Sparks raises an eyebrow at me but doesn't say anything.

When everyone is finished, Sparks gets up and announces, "I want you all to follow me."

We all fall in behind him. He walks out the door and takes a turn toward the docks. The path is gravel and crunches under foot. There are paths leading to other buildings and a common area in the middle that reminds me a bit of home. About the common are trolls, ogres, elves, humans, and even a few dwarves lying on their backs and snoring.

We pass by the commons and enter a row of thatched houses.

Mr. Sparks says, "This is where our couples live."

At the end of the row is a cookhouse. Smoke is coming from two chimneys, one of which is outdoors. There's a large pot the color of soot hanging on a wrought iron hook near the flames. A human man is stirring it with a large wooden spoon.

When we get to the docks, there are several people gathered around nets. They have wooden tools which resemble wooden pins like Ma used to pin up the laundry on a good day. These pins are much larger, and there is twine spooled around the inside of them.

I watch one of the humans, a young woman a few years older than me, press the pin through a hole in the net, then tie off twine to form a new square in the netting.

Mr. Sparks says, "These are our fishers. Today they are mending the nets in preparation for tomorrow's expedition. Chortnel, why don't you lend them a hand. Anna here will teach you what to do.

Anna is the young woman. She smiles up at us. "Hello, I'll be glad to show you what to do, Chortnel. Come sit here next to me and I'll find you a spindle."

Chortnel and baby sit next to Anna. Baby runs down the dock and leaps into the water. Chortnel appears unconcerned by this. Anna hands her one of the thread spindles and begins teaching her the way to tie knots.

Mr. Sparks says, "Grain, Flavor, and Hawk, follow me." We move down the dock, where I see a boat with four ogres standing near. "Right then, you three have rowing practice today. Loam, Gar, Salt, and Rock know how to row. Take that boat there." Sparks points out one of the dwarven boats tied to the dock. "I'll look you up when you return for lunch." He then waves and wanders away.

I look at the four ogres. "What's to keep us from taking this boat around and into the town?"

A breathless elf runs up at that moment. "Sorry I'm late, I see we're all set then? Everyone on to the boat."

The four ogres look at me, and I think they shrug their shoulders. It's so hard to tell what other types of people do sometimes. We all get in the boat.

The elf says, "I'm Golden, and I'll be your teacher today. I want the three of you on the starboard side." She points to the right side of the boat. I take a seat, and Sam sits next to me.

Golden says, "Your dog will have to ride back here with me. He might get hit by an oar where he's sitting now." Golden has her hands on a tiller at the back end of the boat. We all face her.

I pat Sam on the head and point to Golden. "Go sit, Sam." He does as he's told, walking to the back and plopping down next to Golden.

The ogres grab an oar, and the one in front of us shows us how to hold them.

Golden says, "You three beginners watch Salt there and do what he does. We'll take it slow out of the harbor."

We go slow out of the channel, stopping a few times by rowing in reverse when we get too close to the rocks. We pass by the elven watchers with their bows. They don't wave, but I do notice a few nasty looks.

Once on the open water, we start rowing. I follow Salt's example, trying to mimic his rhythm. As we pick up speed, I feel a sense of freedom. It's exhilarating to be moving this quickly through the water. I laugh and hear Grain laugh as well. The ogres aren't nearly as impressed.

We are out in open water, where I can see the harbor town for the first time. Then Golden says, "We have company."

Chapter Twenty-Four

The Sailing Ship

Another pirate boat slices the water past us, towing a strange looking vessel with a dragon's head carved in the bow and a large pole sticking up from the middle. The pole has a cross bar, and from that hangs a long sheet of fabric. It's so startling that I barely notice there's a girl in the pirate boat with her hands bound. She has long black hair, but her back is to me and I can't see her face. They pass us and I watch for a while.

I ask Golden, "What sort of boat is that?"

Golden says, "That's a sailing boat. You've never seen one?"

I shake my head.

Golden says, "They are meant for long distances, for the people of the water who bring goods back and forth from one end of the sea to the other."

"What is a sea?"

Golden chuckles. "The sea is this body of water we are rowing in. It stretches for thousands of kilometers."

We head back to dock. I'm almost sorry to stop for the day. I enjoy being on the water. The simple task of rowing takes up my attention and requires physical exertion. It is simple purpose, and I don't have to think about quests or controlling my new power. The rhythm of rowing with my mates and perfecting our work is a welcome task, free from decisions about killing and using that power.

At the dock, I hop off and tie the boat to the dock post. Grain, Flavor, and the other ogres on our team hop onto the dock, followed by Golden, who inspects the boat, making sure everything is stowed properly before joining us.

Chortnel and her baby are at the nets. The baby clings to her mom, but Chortnel doesn't seem burdened or slowed down by her. The net menders stand when we arrive and join us.

Golden says, "We'll move you out of the new house today and you'll get quarters in the singles barracks." The lights start to fade as Golden leads us to the center of town, where Sparks had led us on his tour and there had been people sleeping all over the place.

There are people here again, only now they're eating and drinking. Some are playing the ogre dice games. Most are just having their meal and talking with their fellow pirates.

I say to no one in particular, "I think I can stay here." I mean it. Life here is simple. There's plenty of food and company and a task to perform every day. A task that takes me out on the water, which I have discovered a fondness for.

Also, since the day we learned to row, there have been no more visions. Maybe the Light found someone else to do its quest. I am just fine with that. Let someone else deal with killing and destroying.

Golden takes us to the singles houses, one for women and the other for men. Trolls occupy one or the other, apparently at their own choice. I find a bunk and stow my stuff away. Sam is whining and looking at me. He's been riding around doing nothing all day and wants to get out and run.

I bend down and ruffle the fur on his head. He licks my face. "Okay boy, let's go fetch the stick." We wander out towards a small patch of trees, where I find a good size stick and heave it. Sam goes bounding off to fetch it and bring it back.

As we play, we go by the new house. I can see the back of the girl who was brought in today. Her long hair runs down to the middle of her back, and she seems to be arguing with Mr. Sparks. I'm not sure that's a good idea, but she's not my problem. I think about her boat and wonder if I can get closer to it to look around.

"Come on Sam, let's go down to the docks." I head off in that direction. Sam bounces in front of me, offering me the stick. I grab it from him and toss it over a small rise. From the other side, I hear Sam barking. I trot up to the top of the rise and see that Chortnel is about to toss Sam's stick back my way. It flies and continues over my head, but I don't watch where it lands. Sam will find it one way or another.

I walk to Chortnel. The baby is sitting on her shoulder, eating a fresh fish. "Your baby looks like she has grown since yesterday."

Chortnel says, "Baby trolls grow very fast, Hawk. It's why they are so cranky when they are born."

I say, "How long will she be like that?"

Chortnel says, "Halle will calm down in a few days. Once they reach about this high." Chortnel holds her hand off the ground about half as tall as she is. "Then they usually slow down."

I say, "Halle looks healthy. I thought you weren't supposed to tell me her name."

Chortnel slaps her head. "You always trick me, Hawk." She then asks, "Where are you headed?"

I say, "I wanted to look over that strange boat that was captured. I've never seen anything like it."

Chortnel says, "I'll go with you. Maybe we can figure a way to take it and escape."

I don't say anything. I haven't really been putting any thought toward leaving this place. Sam runs up with the stick and plops it down in front of Chortnel. I wonder if I should be jealous that he's found someone else to play with.

Halle scrambles down from her perch and picks up the stick and hurls it out over the water.

Sam dances at the end of the dock, barking, then with a good-natured groan, he leaps into the water and chases after the stick.

I say, "You just asked for a bath, Halle. When he comes back, he'll shake himself dry and get us all wet." Halle doesn't reply; instead, she runs and dives into the water. She swims for Sam. I look after them. "She's not going to try and eat Sam again, is she?"

"No worry, Hawk Archer. Halle will find a fish if she gets hungry."

We reach the spot where the boat with the sails is tied. It's larger than I thought, quite a bit larger than the boats Mr. Sparks and crew use. We climb aboard and look around. I move to the bow and look at the dragon carving. It's as large as I am and intricately worked. There are fine contours to it. I run my hand over it, and it feels a little warm.

There is a door about midships. I open it and go down a set of steps into a dimly lit room. There is a bed built into one wall, a closet, and a table with chairs in the center of the room. Light filters in from the outside through round holes carved in the walls on either side of the room, up near the ceiling.

There is not a lot of clutter. The room is neat and tidy, with no ornaments or décor except on the port wall, which is entirely composed of a carving. The carving is of some sort of monster I've never seen before. It has eight legs, and the head is a gray blob in the middle of them. There are round things up and down the inside of the legs.

"What is that?" I point at the wall.

Chortnel frowns and regards it for a moment. She runs her fingers over the carving. She says, "I'm not sure. I once heard of a monster that might look like this. I think it was called a Kraken."

I shudder inside a little. "I hope I never meet one. Do you think they might live around here?"

Chortnel shakes her head. "I doubt it. I've never heard of one being in this area. They are found way out in the depths of the sea, I've heard."

We go back up on deck, where I notice knobs on the pole sticking up out of the middle of the ship. They look like they are meant to allow someone to climb up. So, I climb. I get about halfway up and look down. Chortnel looks much smaller from here. Sam barks and I look out at the dock, where Halle holds the stick in one hand and is devouring a fish held in the other. She rears back as Sam prances and barks, then lets the stick go far out into the water. Sam doesn't hesitate; he rans full tilt to the end of the dock and dives in, then starts paddling towards the stick. I'm glad he's not afraid of the water after what happened to us. It was always something he loved back home.

Chortnel calls up to me, "We should get back. It will be time to eat soon."

I whistle for Sam and Chortnel calls for Halle. I descend, then we walk off the docks towards town. Chortnel asks, "When was the last time you had a vision Hawk?"

I reply, "They stopped the same day we learned to row."

Chortnel doesn't say anything at first, but then says, "So the day that this sailboat and its captain were captured."

I said, "I guess. Anyway, I think maybe the Light got tired of waiting for me and found someone else to bother."

Chortnel says, "You like being a pirate."

"I do. I like it here. I like going out on the water and rowing with the crew. I like coming home tired but satisfied we did something, you know?"

Chortnel nods. "What will you do when you go to capture dwarves? When you have to be a part of the violence again?"

I reply, "I haven't seen any violence. They didn't hurt us when they took us."

Chortnel changes the subject. "You will have to go on the quest, Hawk Archer. You have been chosen. You can't choose not to do this."

I don't reply. Sam and Halle catch up with us and we continue to the village. The cook fire is going, and the smell of the evening meal makes my stomach protest at being empty. We get in line and get our food, then go sit with Grain and the ogres.

The meal tonight is a fish stew. There is a hard crusty black bread with it that is best eaten by soaking it on the stew first. Afterwards, I am offered a drink of grog. I go out to the center field where a lot of other pirates are sitting, throwing the dice, or just talking. Sam comes with me, and after drinking the cup dry, I lie on my back looking up at the dome and the soft pin pricks of the night lights.

I haven't attempted to use my power since we got here. As far as I know Mr. Sparks has no idea what I can do, and I think it's best I keep it that way. I am pretty sure if he were to know just what I could do, he'd get the idea to go attack the town and loot it. I'm pretty sure the only thing holding him back from it now are the town's militia and the cannons trained on the lakeside.

I stroke Sam's head. "We are done with war and blowing things up, Sam. It's a good place here, and who knows? Maybe we'll take one of those sailboats one day and go across the sea." The grog does its work; I close my eyes, smiling and dreaming of seeing far-off places with the friends I've made here.

The next morning, the lights wake me up. I hear people who slept outside groan and stretch. There are a few yawns and quiet talk. Sam isn't next to me, but it doesn't worry me. He's made friends with the village and has probably found someone to feed him or throw a stick.

I yawn and sit up. I'm to be in the lead position today. I stand up, stretch, then head for the cook tent to get breakfast. I get my bowl of oranges and gruel and find Chortnel and Grain sitting with Flavor and her garden.

As I sit, Grain says, "So Hawk, we need to talk about an escape."

I put a spoonful of gruel in my mouth to avoid answering, but she continues. "You've got important work. We can't stay here."

I say, "What if we do? Would it be so bad living here? It's a good life." I put another spoonful into my mouth.

Chortnel shakes her head. "You were chosen. You can't ignore that."

I say, "The Light is ignoring me now. No more visons have grabbed me. I think someone else must have been found."

Grain says, "Do you still have the power?"

I don't answer. I haven't used it, but I can still feel it in me. I think about lying, but I've never been very good at fooling people. I finish my bowl and get up.

"Let's talk about this later. We should get to the docks, I'm at the tiller this morning." I drop the bowl off at the table for used dishes and whistle for Sam. I head to the docks. Grain, Flavor, and Chortnel fall into step with me.

Chortnel says, "The Light might be giving you a reprieve for a reason, Hawk. But your task is for you, I'm sure. The Light chose you, and you won't get out of your duty so easy."

We are at the docks now, and I avoid answering Chortnel. Then I stop, mouth open, staring at the person standing with Mr. Sparks by our boat. She has long black hair and almond eyes. She's the girl from my vision.

Chapter Twenty-Five

Jade Ayu

I close my mouth and compose my face. I look around but no one seems to have noticed my surprise except the girl who, I think, seemed to recognize me as well. I look at her and shake my head just barely, enough so she notices but no one else will.

Mr. Sparks is with a thin, dark skinned young man. The man is younger than Sparks; I'm guessing twenty something. When he smiles, I can see a gold tooth and another with a dark red gem embedded in it. The man's hair is in tight curls down past his shoulders. Each strand is held by several bright colored beads.

Mr. Sparks says, "Fellow pirates, we have a new arrival today. Please welcome Jade Aru. Jade will observe today, I want her to sit with the tiller." He looks around, sees me. "That you, Hawk?"

I say, "Yes, sir." I don't trust myself to say anything more.

"Good, that's good." He looks at his companion. "This is Andre. He will be staying with me for a while."

Andre bows. "It is good to meet you all."

Mr. Sparks puts his arm around Andre. "I'll leave you to it then." He and Andre walk away, whispering and laughing.

I look at the crew, "Well, let's do this."

We board and Jade sits next to me. I can't really talk much as we are facing the six rowers and I don't want anyone to catch on that I know her. I think it must be some sort of weird coincidence, or maybe I had a dream that's similar to a vision. Maybe my mind is playing tricks on me.

Another crew boards the second boat and they lead us out of the channel. I recognize the tiller, but can't remember his name.

A very large bird flies down and lands on the edge of the boat next to Jade. It emits a sort of growl. I've never seen a bird this large.

Jade says, "This is my friend Izzy. She's the smartest bird ever. Izzy, say hi to everyone."

Izzy squawk-growls and flaps her wings. Sam gets up and sniffs the air in the bird's direction.

Chortnel says, "Hello Izzy." The rest of the crew say nothing.

I say, "Nice bird."

Sam moves closer, and Izzy flaps her wings and flies away.

Jade said, "She's shy around strangers." She looks at Sam. "Especially ones that bite."

I say, "Sam wouldn't bite her. He's just curious. Sam, over here, buddy."

Sam comes to me and lays back down at my side.

Jade says, "So we should talk."

I shake my head a little at her. The others are watching us. Chortnel asks, "Talk about what?"

Jade says, "I recognize Hawk, and I'm pretty sure he recognizes me."

Chortnel frowns for a moment and then says, "The visions. You have visions, Izzy?"

I cut in, "We have work to do. Let's just do our patrol and we can talk when we get back to the town."

Chortnel squints at me. I've come to realize that means she doesn't understand something and is trying to concentrate enough to bring understanding. I feel the need to stop Chortnel from saying anything else, so I ask Jade, "Where are you from?"

She replies, "From across the sea in the Chain Islands."

"Have you ever rowed a boat before?"

Jade shakes her head. "Not like this boat. We use sails for the most part and have small one-person rowboats to take us to shore when we need to."

We're heading out of the channel into open water now. There are clouds forming above us, and off in the distance I see a flash. I hope the storm doesn't head our way. Maybe we should head back in.

I say, "I think we should get back to the docks. There's a storm coming." The rowers turn around to see what I'm seeing, but now the storm is gone. The clouds look their normal billowy selves, white and harmless.

Chortnel says, "I don't see any storm, Hawk, are you sure?"

I think about this for a second. It would be an excuse to put us back on the docks but there would be more questions when we get there. Chortnel is going to find out about the vision girl sooner or later.

I decide it should be later. I glance to the other boat, but it hasn't stopped.

I say, "Let's head to the tunnel and see if we can catch a boat."

I turn us in the direction of the tunnel joining this quadrant to the dwarf kingdom of Fuutenhold. I wonder if King Ruuc and Jasmine are well and still scheming. I suppose if they are alive, they are making plans.

I watch the sky out towards the deep part of the sea, but I don't see any more signs of a storm. We get to the entrance and move to the blind side, where we will hear any boat that approaches but they won't see us. The tiller person on the other boat signals me to take the port side if the boat comes from the entrance. This means he will have to move around to the starboard side of any incoming boat. I guess it's just as well—we're a new crew and the other boat has been doing this for a while now. I think most of them have been here for their year and decided they'd stay on anyway. I'm pretty sure that I'll make that same decision when my year is up.

Chortnel opens her mouth to talk but I put a finger to my lips, quieting her. Stealth is a great reason to avoid discussing what I know she wants to discuss. Izzy flies to us and perches near Jade. The bird opens its beak wide and a fish flops out at Sam's feet.

Jade says, "Izzy is making a gift to Sam."

Sam sniffs it and then starts eating by biting off the head.

I say, "Thank you, Izzy. Sam loves fish." I turn to Jade. "Does she bring fish to a lot of people?"

Jade looks at me. "She brings them to me. Sam isn't people .He's your ____," saying a word I've never heard before. I'm about to ask her what that means but just then there is sound coming from the tunnel entrance. The tiller on the other boat signals and begins moving. I wait until they pass in front of us and then signal the rowers to start.

We move into position behind the unwary boat. It's crewed by dwarves and the cargo looks small. That's a good sign, as it means whatever it is, it's too heavy to carry much of it. Precious metals most likely.

As the other boat closes in, I maneuver us to the port side and knock their oars in as my rowers on that side pull in their oars and then pull out their bows. Arrows nocked, we wait and cover the actions of the first boat. We're here for support only. The other tiller person, I wish I could remember his name, I don't know why I can't, gives instructions to the dwarves to move to the bow of the boat. He and his mates board the vessel and pull out restraints.

Then a curious thing happens. The dwarves all leap into the water from the bow and start swimming away back into the tunnel. I think that we may not get captives this time, but then that time thing happens, like with the lightning way back when. Everything slows down as I turn my head towards the boat. The small crates are now blown apart. Splinters of wood and pieces of sharp metal are suspended in the air. The crew that was on the boat is riddled by the flying debris. I look for the energy, and I can see the powerful fire that caused this, but it's too late for me to try and contain it. The energy is nearly spent, and now the air itself is distorted. I can make out a sort of wave made of air pushing the crew on board away from the crates as they are riddled by the debris from the explosion.

The tiller's body is coming apart in red. Two more are a little further from the crates but are also looking like they are going to be killed as well. I have no idea what I can do to stop any of this. If I throw energy that way, it might stop the waves of air, but it would also most definitely kill the crew.

Then I notice beside me that Jade is waving her hands. She's not frozen like the rest of the world but moving just as I am. She glances at me with a curious look, then she extends her hands towards the waves of air. She redirects the waves and the world comes back to normal time.

There's an explosion. The tiller from the other boat is gone except for his boots. He's just gone. Of the others, there were two that were close to the crates, and they are missing parts of their body. I try not to look at them, so I concentrate on the three crew members who are wounded but able to cry out. I put my bow down and shout for my crew to get to them.

Grain has already gone into motion and moved on to the boat. The ogres follow her, and I see Flavor checking on one of the wounded. Chortnel is busy trying to calm Halle. Sam is cowering at my feet. I reach down and stroke his head, whispering soothingly to him. "It's okay Sam. It's over now." Soon, he's wagging his tail and he licks my hand.

I head to the other boat, where Grain is using her power to help one of the injured. Flavor is with one of the others. One of the ogres, I think it's Salt, is helping one of the wounded into our boat. There's a hole in the center, and water is leaking in quickly.

I yell, "We don't have time! We have to move now!"

I pick up the wounded man that Grain is helping, and she is startled back to reality. She gets upset with me. "Hawk, what are you doing? I'm not finished with him."

I say, "The boat is sinking, we have to move now. You can help him once we're safe."

I hold the injured man and step over some debris. My deck on my boat seems a long ways up. I yell for help, and one of the ogres reaches over the side. I hand them the wounded crewmate. I look back to see everyone scrambling up on to my boat as the damaged one sinks further. I leap up as the other boat sinks into the water. Pieces of boat and people float on the surface.

Chortnel says, "We should go after those dwarves and learn what happened."

She pulls me out of my thoughts, and I nod. "Yes, Grain, are the wounded in need of immediate help? Should we head immediately to the docks, or do we have time to get the dwarves who did this?"

Grain has her hands on one of the wounded. She says, "They will be fine. Some have lost blood, but I've stopped the bleeding in time. Get the dwarves if you can."

I turn to Jade and realize that she and I still need to talk, but that will have to come later. "Jade, can you take Grain's place at the oar? Have you watched enough to try it?"

Jade says, "I think I can manage." She moves to Grain's seat and takes up the oar. For the first time I notice that Izzy isn't with us. I hope she's okay, but I'm sure she must have flown away as soon as the explosion happened.

With everyone in place, I direct our boat towards the tunnel entrance. I can't see any swimming dwarves now. They probably were picked up by a waiting boat at the entrance. We move inside the tunnel, but we don't have the torches. I can't go far inside without it becoming completely dark. I look down the tunnel but there's no lights, and no dwarves. I let the rowers continue a short way in, but when the darkness blankets us, I decide to turn and head for the docks.

Mr. Sparks will not be pleased we didn't catch at least one of the dwarves, but there's nothing to be done. The boat that picked them all up must be running without lights too. It would make no sense for us to continue pursuit.

I turn us around and head back to the tunnel entrance. I give Jade a look as the light gives us back the view of each other and things around us. She and I will have to talk. I'm thinking I won't have a choice, just as Chortnel predicted. Whatever the Light has in store, the quest is still there. But at least now I'll have someone else to share it with.

Chapter Twenty-Six

Disputed Property

I steer the boat to the dock, then two of the ogres jump out to tie it up. Grain goes to assist the wounded. We help them walk towards town. When we arrive, we take them to the healer's house. They are taken in by the healers—Grain stays to help them. I go to find Mr. Sparks. Chortnel, Flavor, and her garden come with me, as does Jade.

We find Mr. Sparks on the commons enjoying a meal and grog with his new friend Andre.

I say, "Mr. Sparks, we were attacked this morning."

Mr. Sparks loses his smile for the first time that I know of. "Who attacked you?"

I tell him what happened.

He says, "They all got away and you left the extra boat at the entrance?"

There's a shine in Mr. Spark's eyes now. I don't like it. My fingers tingle with power. Then I hear thunder, loud but still far off. Everyone else looks as well, so I know this time it's real. A storm is coming.

Mr. Sparks says, "Everyone to the common house. We'll have a meeting about this."

Izzy comes flying down and perches on Jade's shoulder. Jade strokes the bird. She says, "Izzy thinks that storm is going to be a bad one."

Mr. Sparks grits his teeth, and I can tell he is trying to control his anger. "A bird is predicting the weather, is it? How novel." He moves towards Jade, and we all are taken by surprise. Before he can actually grab Izzy though, he is thrown backwards as if by a giant hand. He lands on his bottom about five meters away from us.

Jade tells him, "Do not try to touch Izzy. It won't go well with you if you do."

Mr. Sparks gets to his feet with Andre's help. Andre dusts him off, but Sparks pushes him away. He waggles a finger at Jade. "How did you do that?"

"Do what?"

There's burst of bright light, and we all look to the west, out to sea where the storm is. After a count of five or so, there's a crash of thunder. It's still far off, but it's nearer than the last time.

Mr. Sparks looks at the horizon and then looks to all of us. "Go gather everyone you can and tell them to meet at the common house." He looks at Jade. "You will come with me. I need to discuss your ship with you."

I say, "If you are going to talk to her, I'm going to be there." I didn't intend to say anything. It just popped out, as if my mouth and brain belonged to some other person.

Mr. Sparks frowns at me. "Very well, come along, the both of you. I want to show you something."

He leads us to the docks. We walk on wooden planks suspended over the water towards Jade's ship. He asks Jade, "I have heard tales of some sort of special magic, but it was supposedly used in Fuutenhold to free the slaves there. You weren't in Fuutenhold though, were you?"

Jade says, "No, I come from the Chain Islands."

Sparks asks, "Why are you here?"

"I wanted adventure. I was tired of moving goods across the sea from one dock to the other. I wanted to see what else there might be in the world."

Sparks says, "Right then. So how did you knock me on my bottom without so much as a movement of your finger?"

Jade says, "I don't know what you are talking about. You went to touch Izzy and then you tripped."

Sparks shakes his head. We are now in front of Jade's boat. There are two new additions to it. Two cannons have been attached to the decks—one faces over the dragon's head on the bow and the other points astern at the rear of the boat.

Sparks points. "We are going to take over the harbor town."

Jade frowns. "I won't allow these things on my ship. What are they for anyway?"

"They are cannons. We'll be able to fire iron and lead balls at the fortifications of the town and destroy their guns before they can get them up and aimed at us."

"No, I won't allow it. I need this ship to get home again."

There is another flash of brilliant light. This time the thunder is about four seconds after.

Sparks says, "Sorry my dear, but this ship now belongs to the pirate co-op. We have decided to use it to everyone's benefit. You are one of us now, so anything you own belongs to us all."

A light rain starts falling on us. There is another flash, then another. This time the two booms from the outraged sky are only three seconds after.

Mr. Sparks says, "This storm is moving fast. A good thing. It means it won't linger over us for long. But let's get into the common house."

We head for the house. Izzy takes off into the air and Jade calls after her. "Be safe, Izzy!"

Sam finds me and falls into step. Thunder doesn't usually make him nervous, but he whines a bit as we walk to the common house.

When we reach the house, most of the pirate town is there inside. Everyone is talking and the noise is enough to preclude normal speech. There's a small stage set apart at one end of the house, just high enough so anyone standing on it looks over the heads of even the ogres in the audience.

Mr. Sparks climbs the steps to the stage and turns to face everyone. Another flash of lightning lights up the house. The rain is heavier now, and the thunder is only a couple seconds after.

Mr. Sparks raises his hands and says in a loud voice, "Quiet down, quiet everyone, I need your attention." He finds me in the crowd and gestures to me to join him. I don't want to, but I don't see a way to decline without a clash of wills that would be very public. I climb the stairs.

Spark's voice carries surprisingly well out over the crowd. "Your attention. I have a couple announcements to make." Everyone quiets down. "My new friend Andre is a special kind of blacksmith. He makes cannons. I have purchased two of his cannons to be installed on the Bounty, or as some of you may know it, the ship with sails." He makes no mention of Jade, and I wonder how she is taking it. I can't see her in the crowd. Another bright flash, this one leaving an after image on my eyes. It's immediately followed by a large boom that shakes the entire house. Rain hammers on the roof. The wind picks up and begins to howl.

Mr. Sparks speaks louder, getting back the attention of the assembly. "We are going to take over the harbor town using these new cannons. It will be our new headquarters."

The wind picks up some more. A door is blown open. Someone manages to close and secure it. Mr. Sparks goes on. "We will have further discussions regarding those plans in a day or so. I don't want to wait too long before we make this happen, but there is also a new development. Mr. Archer here met with force when trying to acquire a boat today. Hawk, tell the crowd the story."

I clear my throat. The room is lit again by lightning, followed by a huge boom that shakes the house. The rain is pelting the roof like thousands of tiny workers beating on it with hammers.

I speak as loudly as I can. I am surprised that I can speak over the noise of the storm—this room must be designed for sound to carry well from the stage. I tell the crowd what happened and the loss of the other crew. I want to give them names, but I haven't had time to find out who they were yet. I just skip over that part completely. There will be questions, and hopefully Sparks will handle that part.

When I'm finished, Sparks says, "Because of this aggression, I fear we have no choice but make a couple new rules."

Lightning flashes, thunder roars. I think that the thunder should start to lag again as the storm moves off, but it doesn't, the flashes and booms are nearly at the same time. Again, the house is shaken.

Sparks says, "It seems even the Light is angry about these new events."

There's an uneasy chuckle from parts of the crowd.

"In light of this aggression, I've decided that from now on, no fewer than four boats will go out to acquire the dwarven boats coming from the tunnel. Secondly, to keep safe, we kill any dwarf that crews on these boats."

Now there's a murmur in the crowd. I'm stunned. I have sworn to myself that I won't kill again unless absolutely necessary. I can't allow any leeway in that. I won't kill dwarves simply because their boat might blow up.

Someone from the crowd yells, "Kill the little blighters! They dare to kill some of us, they deserve death!"

I can see Chortnel. She's shaking her head sadly. The crowd is mostly in favor of the new rule, and there are several cheers aimed at Mr. Sparks. I don't like this new development at all.

There's another flash and this time I can hear something being torn. The noise is soon overwhelmed by a loud boom which again shakes the walls. Then all the doors blow open. Jade comes to the stage and gestures for me to come down. Sparks is directing a few people to get the doors closed again, so I hop off the stage and go to Jade.

She speaks into my ear, "I haven't seen you use the power yet, but you must have it. Together we should try to calm this storm."

I think about telling her I don't have any power because I don't want to use it, but maybe harnessing and controlling the lightning will not be as overpowering as creating explosions is. I nod to her, and we hold hands as we head for a door. Outside, the rain drenches us the moment we step out. Jade tugs me towards the horizon and she raises her free hand to the sky. A bolt of lightning is being formed as the rain and wind stop for me suddenly.

I look up and can see the drops suspended in air. Out on the commons, a tree has been split right down its center. I can see smoke being blown by the wind, now stopped and not moving. The lightning is moving, however. It is snaking towards us, branching right and left but always moving back on track in our direction.

I reach out and grab it, and just as I do, Jade does something to the wind, I think, because I can feel her power.

Then a vision takes me. I am far up in the air looking down at the sea. There's a pie-shaped island with docks at the north, east, south, and west. In the middle I see a hill, and in the hill is a cave tunnel. I can see rusted iron rails leading into it. The voice says "Come" in my head. It's faint this time, but I have no doubt it's going to get louder.

My heart sinks. That's it. If Spark's new orders didn't drive me away from this place, the knowledge of another vision is the last incentive I need. I'll have to leave now.

I direct the bolt of lightning out to sea, then I feel the wind calming. I look at Jade. She's looking at me with her calm almond eyes. She says, "You saw the cave tunnel?"

I nod. "It's like the first vision I had, only in a different place this time."

The rain is back to just sprinkling now and I can see light through the clouds.

"You had a vision like this one before?"

"Yes, didn't you?"

She shakes her head. "No the first vision I had was of your face and the voice told me to find you."

I ask, "How did you know to come here?"

She shrugs. "I'm not exactly sure. I just knew the direction I had to sail in and came."

I notice we are still holding hands, so I let go. "We'll have to figure out a way to take your ship back."

"It won't be easy getting it out of the channel."

I think about this. "Let's go inside. Tonight, we'll get together with Chortnel, Grain, and Flavor to talk about what to do."

I smile as pieces of a plan start to fit together for me.

Chapter Twenty-Seven

The Escape Plan

After supper, I take a stroll. Chortnel comes with me, and the rest are instructed to follow after waiting at least ten minutes. Halle rides on Chortnel's shoulders. She is more than a quarter of Chortnel's size now. Every time I see her, it seems she is devouring fish. Sam sniffs hopefully in her direction but is ignored.

Chortnel says, "We can't allow the dwarves to be killed."

I say, "All we can do is refuse to do it ourselves. How can we stop the rest of them?"

Chortnel looks at me. "You could use your power."

I sigh. "I don't know how to control it. Something happened to it when I was a slave."

"You did something to the lightning, didn't you? During this last storm?"

"Yes, but that wasn't directing power, it was just moving power that was already there."

"You should try. It's wrong to kill without warning, and it will start a war with Fuutenhold. You know Ruuc. He will send war parties to wipe out the pirates."

"If we interfere, Mr. Sparks will stop us." I scratch my head. "I don't like the look of him. There's something about his eyes that aren't right."

Chortnel says, "He's mad."

I say, "He doesn't seem to be crazy to me. He's nice enough."

"He's the worst kind of mad. He's not a drooling gibbering kind, but a cold calculating kind that hides it well."

We come to the giant boulder that marks the shoreline. Water laps at the bottom of it. We climb and sit, waiting for the rest to join us. The lights dim in the first fading. It will be dark soon. I stand and look back to see if the others are in sight yet but don't see them.

Chortnel says, "Try using the power. Try sending just a small amount into the water."

I turn and face the sea. I can feel the power building in my fingertips. I strain to harness it, to hold it back and release just a small amount. I aim at a place in the sea, and it erupts in a huge geyser that travels fifty meters into the air.

Chortnel strokes her chin, looking at the explosion, then glancing at the shoreline. She says, "I have an idea."

She climbs down off the rock and grabs a bone-white, gnarled piece of driftwood half buried in beach sand. She pulls it out and wipes it clean. Halle decides she's ridden long enough and climbs down from her mother, then sets off for the shore. She dives in, and Sam barks, then jumps from the boulder directly into the water.

I watch as Chortnel climbs back up and sits next to me. She hands me the gnarled piece of wood. It has weight to it, but not water weight.

It's completely dry. I try to scratch the surface, but it's hard as a bone. I heft it. It's about a meter long.

I ask, "What am I supposed to do with this?"

"Try using it to channel your power. Send the power through this staff and then into the water."

"I think you've been spending too much time near Mr. Sparks. His craziness has rubbed off on you."

"Just try it, Hawk."

I stand up and concentrate. The power builds in my hand and I think it into the staff. I feel it move and I control the flow of it before sending a beam towards a spot away from Sam and Halle. A splash of water leaps into the air. Far smaller than the huge geyser I'd created before.

I hold my breath, not wanting to believe just yet. I send another bolt, this time concentrating on sending only a little more power. This time there's a bigger shower but still far smaller than the first try.

I laugh, then grab Chortnel and hug her.

"How in the world did you think to do this?"

Chortnel shows me her chilling grin. It no longer frightens me, but it will always be a little off-putting, I think. "I was thinking about how lightning bends and twists. It seems to follow the easiest path when it comes through the air. I thought maybe there might be something you could use to channel the energy and harness it by changing its path."

"That makes no sense to me."

"You aren't a troll."

The others arrive. They climb up the boulder and stand near us.

Grain says, "What's the piece of driftwood for?"

I tell her, "Chortnel's idea. I can use it to control how much power I use. Watch this."

THE WIZARD OF FIRE

I raise the staff and send just enough power to spray Sam and Halle with water.

Jade says, "Can you use it to increase your power?"

I say, "That's a great question. Let me try."

I raise the staff and feel a surge of power moving through the staff. I aim it far out to sea. A huge eruption causes water to burst into the air in a giant fountain. I think it must be at least 100 meters high, but it's hard to tell from a distance.

Flavor says, "You could take over the harbor town if you wanted all by yourself."

The other ogres grunt in assent.

I say, "I don't want to hurt anyone. I have killed, and I don't like it even when it's necessary."

Flavor doesn't respond to that. Chortnel says, "Let's talk about getting Jade her ship back and getting out of here."

I lay out my plan. The others have questions. We talk, discuss, change, and rework the plan to everyone's satisfaction. Now the last of the evening lights change to the night lights. It's dark, and getting off the boulder is going to be tricky. But I have an idea.

I raise the staff above my head and concentrate just a little power above its tip. A soft blue globe of energy appears. I make it stronger, and light shines down on to the ground.

Grain says, "You're learning all sorts of things."

Everyone scrambles off the boulder. I whistle for Sam and climb down. He runs up and shakes himself dry, getting the rest of us wet in the process. Halle scrambles up, a fish in each hand. The head is gone on one of them.

We walk back to the commons and Chortnel agrees to wake us all in a couple hours. We'll execute our plan in the middle of the night.

I want to use the staff some more, but I know I need to get some sleep, and besides, I don't want it to be common knowledge what I can do just yet. I use the staff as a walking stick and hope it doesn't raise too many questions.

As I like to do most nights when it's not raining, I find a tree and lean back against it. Sam puts his head in my lap as I look up at the dome lights. I wonder about my quest. I wonder about where that island cave leads. Then I sleep.

Someone shakes me gently awake. Chortnel whispers in my ear, "Hawk, it's time. Get up."

I groan softly and sit up. I wipe the sleep from my eyes and yawn. "Is everyone else ready?"

Chortnel says, "Yes, Grain and Flavor are on their way to round up the archer elves. Jade is on her way to slip into the water and climb her way up into her ship."

"Let's go then." I stand up and start walking. Chortnel grabs the staff she'd given me. "Don't forget this."

I grab it. "Thanks."

We meet with the rest of the ogres at the dock and move quietly. They find a boat and start to release it. Chortnel and I move to the ship. I begin untying the moorings.

A voice startles me from behind. "What might you be doing there, Hawk Archer?"

I turn around and look into Mr. Spark's overbright eyes. He's carrying a torch and I have no idea how I missed him. I start to send a little power at him, just enough to push him into the water, but six of his elven archers appear and with nocked arrows in the bows, they surround Chortnel and me.

I'm not sure I can channel enough energy to knock them all out before at least one of them shoots us, so I remain still and don't say anything.

Sparks says, "So, out with it. What are you doing with this ship in the middle of the night?"

I say, "We were going to take it out in open water and try out the cannons."

Mr. Sparks chuckles and wags a finger in my face. "Don't try to sparkle the eyes of a sparkler, Mr. Archer."

I'm not sure what that means, but Chortnel says. "Why don't you just tell him not to lie to a liar?"

Mr. Sparks grins at Chortnel. "Trolls. You know I'd thought at first, we'd just kill any of you who tried to join us. You're all so literal minded and not easily persuaded." He grins at Chortnel. "But in the end, I was convinced that all should be welcome."

I think I hear a noise from the other side of the ship. Like water dripping off a person, but maybe that's wishful thinking.

Mr. Sparks turns to me. "What is that piece of driftwood for? You're far too young to need a cane, and it doesn't look as though you mean it to be a weapon."

I say, "Chortnel found it and said I'd look good using it. Since it was a gift, I thought I'd give it a go."

The elves move to tie the ogres hands behind their backs, then I say, "But I have discovered it makes a decent weapon." While the elves move closer, they pass Mr. Sparks. It's what I was waiting for, and I tap the staff on the dock. Energy leaps out and touches the elves and Mr. Sparks. They all fall to the dock, unconscious.

The ogres get busy tying them all up. I hear the ripping of cloth as they tear garments to make gags with. When they are all tied, I help Chortnel grab one of the elves. The ogres each grab another, and

Flavor picks up Mr. Sparks. We board one of the boats and lay them all in a line at the bottom. I grab a tarp and pull it over them all.

Chortnel says, "That should keep them out of our wake for a bit."

From the deck of the ship, Jade appears and waves to us. In the dim light, she's not much more than a shadow on the background of night lights, but then Grain steps next to her with a lantern.

I say, "Alright then, let's get on with it." Two of the ogres join Chortnel and me. We climb aboard one of the boats and release it from the dock. Flavor and the other three ogres do the same with another boat. We each move into position on either side of ship. Grain and Jade toss us lines and we secure them to the sterns of both boats.

With only four oars per boat, we don't have enough people to have anyone on the tiller. Grain stands in the bow of the ship and relays to us instructions as to what direction we need to row in. Sam sits by the tiller, and I wish I'd thought of a way to train him to move it, but it's too late now.

From the stern of Jade's ship, I hear Jade say, "I can't see very well where we are headed. I need you to guide me, Grain."

Grain says back to her, "I'll do my best. I have to guide the boats as well." She calls down to us. "Row to the starboard."

We pull heavy on the port side oars and the boat moves to the right. She calls down, "That's good, now straighten out." We all pull equally. I can't see the sides of the channel. I wish there was enough light, but the darkness can work for us as we move past the elven posts above. I'm hoping that many of the elves that would normally be on duty up there are tied up in the boat with Mr. Sparks. We won't know for sure for a few minutes yet.

"Pull port!" Grain calls down to us. She calls back to Jade, "Steer port a bit!" After a few seconds, she calls out again to go straight.

Then she calls to all of us, "We're coming on the first turn ahead. We are close to the port side of the channel." We continue rowing and after a bit Grain calls again. "Okay, pull starboard now." We all pull harder on the portside oars to change course. She calls back to Jade, "Stay the course, Jade, I'll let you know when to steer starboard."

We continue and I can see water lapping at the rocks on the port side of the channel. It seems like we've turned completely around, but Grain hasn't told us to stop turning port side yet. Finally, she calls down to us. "Okay, pull straight now!"

She calls back to Jade. "Steer starboard!"

Something whizzes by my head. An arrow sticks in the aft wall, behind the tiller. Another whizzes by, then one of the ogres grunts in pain. Several plopping sounds tell us there are arrows hitting the water around us.

My hope was unfounded. There are elven archers on the perch above.

Chapter Twenty-Eight

Mr. Sparks is not Happy

I don't want to stop rowing long enough to grab my staff, but if I use the power without it, I might kill all the elves up there. I know that's what they are trying to do to us, but I made a vow and I'm going to stick to it. A few more arrows plop into the water near us. I hear another grunt from the other boat from an ogre who must have taken an arrow.

I have to do something. I start to stow my oar when I feel a breeze. There are no more plops in the water or whizzing arrows shooting by. Jade must have used her power to do something.

Grain calls down, "Pull starboard!" I pick my oars again and pull hard on the port side. We begin turning into a bend in the channel. As we move across the bow of the ship, I look back and see lights bobbing behind us.

I call up to Grain. "We're being followed."

Grain calls back, "Yes, Jade has seen them."

Pulling the ship along is slow business. I second guess whether or not we should have taken just one boat, but Chortnel had been very clear about needing two boats. We straighten out when Grain calls back to Jade to steer starboard. The lights disappear, but they are definitely coming closer as the bow of the ship obscures their view.

There is one more bend before we hit open water. I call up to Grain, "How close are they?"

Grain calls back, "Jade says they are hanging back. She thinks they know she can call the wind on them."

I wonder about this. Why bother chasing us if they don't intend on stopping us? I can't worry about that now though. I pull as hard as I can on the oars, and then the boat leaps forward. The line to the bow goes slack and the ship starts to catch up to us.

Grain calls back, "That's enough. We don't want to ram our boats." The ship slackens and I feel the tug on the boat. I definitely get the sensation that we are moving faster.

Grain calls down to pull port, and we pull harder on the starboard oars. We're at the final bend now. As we turn the ship, I can see the lights again. There's a flash, then the sound of an explosion. A few rocks on the channel wall fly up in the air. I wonder if Mr. Sparks has found someone else with the power, but then Chortnel says, "They have cannons on the boats."

Another report sounds and a few seconds later water sprays up on the starboard side of the ship. I hear Jade call out "Izzy! No!" The ship stops moving forward and we all slow down again. The ogres and I keep rowing. I hear two more explosions from the direction of the chasing boats, then there is a splintering crash from the back of the ship.

I call out, "What happened?"

Grain doesn't answer right away as she disappears from her post. We continue rowing. Glancing over my shoulder, I think I can make out the mouth of the channel. We are almost to open water. I'm not sure if that will make much difference, but maybe if Jade can open the sails, the ship can move away and I can grab my staff and stop Mr. Sparks before they can do any further damage.

Another report sounds, then a loud splash can be heard on the starboard side of the ship. Grain comes back and calls down to us. "Jade is trying to protect Izzy. She can't use her wind on the boats as long as Izzy is harassing them, and she's afraid they will shoot arrows at her."

Then there is an agonized shout from Jade. "Izzy!"

Grain goes out of sight for a moment as two more cannon shots are fired. One lands in the water on the port side, and a splintering crash tells me another one has hit the ship. I don't know how much damage the ship can take and still stay afloat, but I decide I had better get in the fight. I call to the other boat to unlash the ropes. We get ourselves free of the ship and I call out to Flavor to move as quickly as she can to the harbor town. I call up to Grain. "What's going on now?"

Grain replies, "Izzy is hurt. Jade is using the wind to bring her to us. The boats are pursuing and getting ready to fire again."

I tell Chortnel, "Grab the tiller and bring us around. We need to get behind the ship so I can use the staff."

Chortnel moves to the tiller and the ogres start straining on the oars. I grab my staff and head for the bow. Two more reports from the cannons—one hits the ship again, the other falls towards the sea on the port side. I can't see the ball coming, but I hear it, then I try to slow everything down like when I'm looking at lightning. It doesn't work. The ball keeps falling. I aim the staff at the noise and let go a broad stream of fire. The ball hits it and disappears in a puff of smoke.

We round the rear of the ship and I stand in the bow, my arms raised, my staff pointing to Mr. Sparks and company. I let go of the fire again and lightning shoots out. It lands in front of the boats and a geyser erupts into the air. The boats are thrown off course, but they don't capsize. In the torchlight I can see Mr. Sparks giving instructions to the rowers. His friend Andre stands in the bow of the other boat, aiming the cannon at us. I can see a bright light and I hear a whistle in the air. I wave my staff and a wall of fire travels towards the boats. The cannon ball pierces the wall. It comes through on fire but isn't stopped. I aim energy directly at it, then it explodes in the air.

I call up to Jade, "If you have Izzy, then head for the docks of the harbor town." I hope the ship isn't damaged beyond the point that it can move. My concerns are answered when the ship lurches forward and heads around the bend toward the harbor town.

Mr. Sparks gets his boat righted and I see the flash of light from the cannon, then hear the boom. I throw up another wall of flame. The lead ball pierces it and I see it is going to fall far short of the ship. I raise my staff and send another bolt of lightning into the water in front of the boats. The water capsizes the boat Andre is in, but Mr. Sparks keeps coming, it seems.

I am proven right with another flash from the cannon. I hear the whistle of the lead ball. Another flash of fire, and I can see it heading right for our little boat. I wonder at the precision it must take to aim and fire on such a small target. Maybe he just got lucky. I raise my staff and shoot energy that intercepts the ball before it can land.

I tell Chortnel, "Let's row for the town now." She pulls on the tiller, then we come about. As we head towards the ship, I turn in the bow and face Mr. Sparks' boat. It looks like it's still moving toward us. I can see Mr. Sparks in the bow, fiddling with the cannon. Soon, another cannon ball is on its way after a muzzle flash and a boom.

I use the same trick to find and destroy this one as well. Coming up behind Mr. Sparks, I see the lights of four other boats. They are gaining on Mr. Sparks, and I hope they don't all have cannons on them.

I use my staff to shoot fireballs above the town, hoping they will see and come man their own cannons. Of course, they might target us if they do, but I hope that between Jade and I, we can deflect anything they shoot at us. Once the pirates get close, the town's cannons should target them.

Nothing happens at first, and I turn back when I hear another cannon shot being fired. There's a whistling sound and I throw up a flame wall, but it's too late. The ball hits the boat at the water line, and water gushes in.

"Sam, jump!" I say as I dive into the water. Chortnel and the ogres jump in as well and we all start swimming for shore. I have a memory of swimming in the dark tunnel, holding on to Sam. I am about to call out for him when I feel his nose nudging my face.

"There you are, good boy. Time for you to pay me back for keeping you afloat last time." I hold a patch of fur and my staff in one hand, and with the other I paddle. "Take us to shore, Sam."

It doesn't take us long to reach the shoreline. Lucky for us, the beach is sandy here and we climb out of the water and sit, looking out to the docks. The ship has rounded the short channel and the mast can be seen moving deeper into the docking area. There's no sign of the other boat. I can only hope they were able to get into the dock as well.

The pirates have turned and paddled away. They are no match for the town's cannons at this point. The torches of the archer boats fade away as they move towards Seacove.

I say, "We should get to the docks and see how bad the ship was damaged."

The night lights turn to dawn as we get up to walk to the docks. Sam growls. I notice a group of people headed our way. Some have swords, some have bows. When they reach us, I can see most of them are human and have eyes like Jade's. Two of the archers are elven.

One the men, tall and with a shaved head, is holding a sword. He says, "I think you'll be coming with us now. Let me have that staff and come along peacefully so we don't have to hurt you."

I am not about to give up my staff. I just recently obtained it and it's becoming a part of me. I decide I can afford to put on a little show for these people. Why not? I'm the Chosen of the Light. I can't remember if that's the right title, but it won't matter.

I bang my staff in the sand. It sort of loses any effect, as the sand simply muffles the sound. Still, I transfer power to the tip, and it glows at first and then sparks. I aim it at the speaker's feet and shoot a small amount of energy that makes the sand erupt to about his knees.

I say, "I'm the Chosen of the Light and have a quest to fulfill. We mean you no harm, but I can't allow you to make us your prisoners."

The speaker looks unsure now, but he says, "If you don't come with us, we will attack you."

I look him in the eye. "I am Hawk Archer. What is your name?"

"I'm Paul. Paul Yee, militia general of Harbortown. You will be our prisoners. Now come quietly or we attack."

I hit Paul with a quick bolt. He's knocked to the ground and his soldiers pull back on their bows. I raise the staff and the people with bows are knocked to the ground as well.

"We don't come to do harm. We only want to repair our ship, which was damaged by the pirates. If you try to harm us, we will defend ourselves."

I go to Paul and offer him a hand. He takes it and stands up, then brushes himself off. Paul eyes me, then tells his soldiers to stand down.

He says, "The pirates attacked you? That ship was seen going into Seacove. Aren't you all part of Mr. Sparks' army?"

"We were a part, but Mr. Sparks has made new rules, and a war with the dwarves from Fuutenhold will happen any day now. We want no part of killing and fighting. We have a quest that takes us across the sea, and we need the ship repaired so we can complete it."

Paul offers me his hand. I grasp his arm with mine and we hold like that for a few seconds. He says, "Follow me. We'll talk with the village elders about getting your ship repaired."

The dawn lights get a little brighter as we start up the beach, but then we hear cries for help behind us. A half dozen dwarves are swimming our way. Behind them, staying just out of range, is one of the archer boats.

The Dwarven War has begun.

Chapter Twenty-Nine

Harbortown

Paul and his militia fetch the dwarves from the water. Two are injured with arrows sticking in them.

One of them says, "My name is Croat. We were on our way here with a delivery of gems when the pirates attacked. We had three boats total, two of them with archers ready to fight back. There was a battle and the two war boats held back, blocking the pirates while we rowed for your harbor. Our friends in the archer boats were all killed. The pirates came after us shooting arrows," Croat stopped and coughed, catching his breath before continuing. "We were sure they were going to kill us too, then one of the boats shot something at us. There was a loud boom, a whistling noise, and something crashed through the floor of our boat. It sank, and the pirates took off."

Croat stopped to cough. "I don't know why they wanted to kill us. Usually, they would just take the boat and let us go."

I said, "One of your boats blew up earlier, killing six pirates when they were on board."

Croat looked at me, confused. "I don't know anything about that. We were told the pirates had to be stopped. That's why we came in three boats this time, but I think we'll need to bring more."

I look at Paul. "A war is coming."

Paul nodded. "Let's get everyone to the healer. We can talk to the council about what to do after that."

We follow Paul, the ogres helping the wounded as best they could. We now have two ogres and two dwarves with arrows sticking out of them. I hope that Izzy is okay. Grain is with the others, so at least she could be tended to right away.

The healer isn't far, and we bring the wounded inside. The rest of us stay out and wait for the meeting with the council. Paul is with us.

"Those pirates have been a pain for a while now," he says. "That Mr. Sparks tried to come here and tell us he wanted to be a part of our community, but I could tell he was looking to take over running our town. Something's not right with him."

I say, "You're a smart man, Mr. Yee. He's got an idea that he can kill people without much thought about it."

Paul says, "It's General Yee. If Mr. Sparks thinks he can take over our town, he is not right in the head."

I say, "He was going to use Jade's ship. He had a friend of his put cannons on it. He planned to attack you at night."

Paul says, "The ship that just came into our docks?"

I nod. "Yes, and I want to go there and see how my friends are doing. A large bird belonging to the captain of the ship was injured, I think, and the ship was hit by cannon twice."

Paul turns to one of his soldiers. "Go tell Jim Seo we will meet with him after we access the ship in docks."

The soldier bows and runs off. Paul turns to us. "Let's go see about your ship."

I look for Sam and see that he's found something interesting to smell. I whistle and he comes on the run. I pat his head. Paul leads us to the docks.

Paul asks me, "What is your relationship with Mr. Sparks?"

I know he's asking me if I'm a pirate. I suppose I could make something up about being captured. That is what happened, but I don't see how I can make an elaborate lie without it being full of holes, so I decide on the truth.

"We were coming from the northwest quadrant, and the pirates captured us. We were told we'd either join them or be sold into slavery." Paul nods at this as I continue. "So, we joined him, my friends and I." I clear my throat and look at Paul. "I'll be honest, I enjoyed my time as a pirate. It was an easy life up until the dwarves blew up a boat and killed some of my mates. After that, things got very serious very quickly. Sparks, as you said, isn't quite right in the head. He decided to kill any dwarf that came through the tunnel. I spoke against it, and he didn't like it. When I saw what he was doing to Jade's ship, I knew we had to do something. So my friends and I tried to escape quietly with the ship. He was waiting for us. We got away, but well, you pretty much know the rest."

Paul nods. We are on the docks and go to where the larger ships are birthed. There are several as large as Jade's, and from here I can see several more anchored in the distance. They have three masts rather than one like Jade's ship. I think they probably are too large to put into the docks here.

Jade and Grain are walking toward us. Jade holds Izzy, who has a bandage wrapped around her middle. There's a guard with them, along with three humans with bows, but the bows are slung over their shoulders, and it doesn't look like my friends are being held captive.

I say, "How is Izzy?"

Jade says, "She will be fine. The arrow didn't pierce anything vital, but I hope to train her not to be so aggressive. Next time she might not be so lucky." Jade strokes the bird's head as she speaks.

"What shape is the ship in? Can it sail?"

Jade says, "Not without repair. We'd not make it a hundred kilometers in the shape she's in right now."

I say, "This is Paul Yee, he's the general of the town's militia. Paul, this is Jade Ayu and Grain."

Paul bows and Jade returns it to him.

Jade says, "Your people have been kind, General. I thank you for your hospitality."

"We offer aid to any who come as friends. I am told you have cannons on board your vessel?"

Jade says, "Yes general, and I would thank you to remove them as soon as you can. I don't like having weapons on board."

Paul says, "You aren't afraid of pirates? Of being attacked?"

I say, "We have other ways of dealing with aggression."

Paul nods to me. "Your staff is one. I take it Ms. Ayu is another?"

Jade says, "General, I hope we can come to some arrangement for repairs to my ship. I checked my hold, and there are still a few crates of island spices there we can trade for what we need."

Paul says, "We'll discuss it with the council. I'll have some workers sent to retrieve the cannons in the meantime. Please, follow me." He turns to one of his soldiers. "Mi Yae, please go to the master blacksmith and inform him of the task that needs to be done." The soldier bows and leaves.

Paul says, "Now, if you will follow me, we will have refreshments and discuss our next steps."

We follow him. I look at Chortnel, wondering why she's so quiet. Normally she would have something to say in any conversation. Then I notice that Halle is not with her. "Chortnel, where's Halle?"

Chortnel is startled as though she'd been in deep thought. "I think she's gone fishing again. She'll find me when she wants to." It surprises me how nonchalant the troll is about her child. A human wouldn't let a baby out their sight.

We arrive at a large house with squares of gray tar covering a sloped roof. The walls are white with dark brown braces forming squares. We are taken inside and directed to a table where we all sit.

Several sprites, with coloring much like Drafa's in Seacove, bring bowls and cups to us. The bowl in front of me has chunks of some sort of fish along with dark green leafy stuff. I take up the spoon set by it and sip. It's hot and spicy and tastes delicious. I hadn't realized how hungry I was until my mouth hurt as the saliva poured out at the taste of the soup.

A tall elven woman comes in dressed all in the color of the sea. She stands a good two meters tall and towers over the other people with her. She joins us at the table and sprites bring her a bowl and cup as well.

Before sitting she says, "I am Lian Seo, wife of Jim Seo and co-leader of Harbortown. I welcome you to our village." She bows.

I decide I should probably stand. I clear my throat, wipe my hands on my thighs, and say, "I am Hawk Archer, a vision quester of the Light. We thank you for your kind hospitality." I bow awkwardly and nod to Chortnel. She stands and introduces herself, followed by Flavor and the other ogres who weren't injured, then Grain and lastly Jade, who introduces herself as also being of the Light and on a quest.

Lian sits, then sips broth. She sets her spoon down and looks first at me, then at Jade. "What quest are you on?"

I say, "The world is breaking down. We have been called to a quest we hope will fix it. Jade and I have powers given to us by the Light, and we are also given visions. We must sail far across the sea to an island where there is a tunnel to another place, possibly another quadrant. The Light calls us there."

A human comes in and whispers in Lian's ear. She stands and says, "Please excuse my rudeness. I am told there is an important visitor just arrived from Fuutenhold." She bows and hurries out.

I don't really mind as now I can finish this delicious soup without interruption. Chortnel says, "What do you think is going on?"

Jade says, "Fuutenhold wants Harbortown to support them in fighting the pirates."

I spoon soup into my mouth. I really don't care about the pirates or Fuutenhold anymore. Let them fight between themselves. I doubt Harbortown is going to aid either side. With their guns and militia, I doubt either the pirates or the dwarves are going to want to antagonize the people here.

Flavor says, "I'm more interested in how long it will be to repair Jade's ship and if we are all going on this quest."

I burp politely and wipe my face on my sleeve. "Do you want to go, Flavor?"

Flavor looks at me. She doesn't speak at first. I know ogres are slow in processing their thoughts. She looks at the rest of the ogres. Two, Salt and Gar, are bandaged. Salt has a crease in his forehead, and Gar's mouth is a little wider than the others.

There seems to be some unspoken conversation between them all. Flavor turns back to me and says. "We would like to help you on your quest, Hawk. We think such an important thing needs to be done even if it makes us famous."

"Why would you not want to be famous?"

Flavor says, "Ogres don't much care for attention. It's our nature to stay away from such things."

I don't have a reply. Just then, Lian returns with several dwarves. One of them looks familiar.

That one says, "Hello Hawk, Chortnel, Grain, the rest of you."

She is female, and since there's only one female dwarf I've met, I can guess who it is.

I say, "Hello Jasmine. What brings you here?"

Lian says, "Jasmine wanted to greet you. She is here as representative of King Ruuc to talk with us about the pirate problem."

Jasmine says, "Yes, and I was hoping to enlist your help as well, Hawk."

I say, "I'm glad to see you and Ruuc have come to an agreement. How are things in Fuutenhold?"

"Fuutenhold is adjusting. We have many people, former slaves, who have left, but enough remain to keep the mining going. Of course, they have a voice now, someone to speak for them."

"Anyone I know?"

"I think so. Truut and Dolain."

I nod. "Truut the troll, and Dolain the elf. Well, I wish you all the best. I'm sure your city will be prosperous." That sounds weak when I say it, not nearly as sophisticated as it did in my head.

Jasmine says, "I will pass on your wishes to Ruuc. We are hoping you will help us defeat the pirates."

"Me? I don't want any part of more fighting, thank you. We are going to get my friend's ship repaired and then be on our way."

I glance over at Jade, and we are both taken into a vision. I can see her looking at me as the rest of the world looks like it sinks under water. Jasmine says something but I don't understand it. The vision of the island floats in front of me and the words "Come" are whispered in my ear.

Chapter Thirty

The Pirate Problems

When the vision fades, I hear Chortnel asking that we be left alone to discuss the issues. People file out of the room, leaving Chortnel, Grain, Jade, the ogres, and myself, along with Sam and Izzy.

I ask Chortnel, "What is it you want to discuss?"

"Mr. Sparks is a real problem. He will continue to be a danger both to Harbortown and to Fuutenhold if something isn't done."

"But it's not our fight. We have been delayed far too often as it is."

Chortnel says, "We can't leave until the ship is repaired, and who knows how long that might be? It could take weeks to make the repairs."

Jade says, "I think it will be about a week. The damage is pretty straightforward, and Harbortown has the materials and tools available."

"So we have a week," Chortnel replies. "Are you going to sit around and do nothing for a week, Hawk Archer?"

When she uses my full name, she reminds me of Ma. You'd think I'd resent that, but the longer I go without seeing my mother, the more I seem to miss her. I sigh. Chortnel is right. I'm not someone to sit around and do nothing.

"Okay," I say, "so we give it a week. If we can rid the world of Mr. Sparks and company by then, all is good. If not, we still leave as planned. Do you all agree?"

Chortnel nods in agreement, then the rest follow.

I stand. "Alright, let's go inform the others."

Chortnel goes to the door and beckons the town and Fuutenhold representatives back to the room. When everyone is settled, I began. "We are grateful for the help from Harbortown and the repairs. We also recognize that the pirates are a dangerous threat and are only going to be more so to all of you. We have decided to give a week to stopping Sparks and his pirates while repairs are being made to Jade's ship."

Jim Seo says, "We need a plan. The channel into Seacove is well guarded."

"There's the hidden cove on the other side," Jade points out.

Jim says, "There's no way to land boats there. The beach is all rock. It will be slippery and hard to navigate."

I say, "Can we somehow sneak up on the archers?"

"I've been thinking about that," Paul Yee says. "Normally we wouldn't be able to get close enough to shoot them with bows, but maybe we can sneak by them at night."

I look at my friends. "Has anyone tried doing that?"

They all shake their heads. I look at Yee and say, "I have no idea how well guarded the channel is at night, but I think Sparks is smart enough to have torches or something to light up the channel."

Jasmine says, "Before we do that, let's make sure I can get more dwarves here to help. If you can send a few boats to the tunnel entrance tomorrow night, I'll bring a force with me."

Paul says, "We don't have a lot of boats set up like that. We rely mostly on our town defenses to keep the pirates away. We don't have a fighting force to speak of."

"Just bring as many as you can," Jasmine says, "and make sure you include these two." She nods to Jade and me.

The meeting breaks up. I decide to go see the ship for myself. Chortnel and Jade come with me.

As we walk, I say, "I don't like how they are relying on our power to overcome the pirates."

Jade says, "I think we are going to deal with that no matter where we find ourselves."

Sam lopes ahead of us, then stops and sniffs at something on the path. When we catch up, he's off again until the next smell that interests him.

"Well then, let's make a promise that we are not going to let anyone know about our powers unless we have to."

Jade and Chortnel agree. I know asking the troll to keep a secret is pretty silly considering her past, but it will have to do for now.

We arrive at the ship, and Jade points out the damage. The ship has been lifted out of the water and put into what she calls drydock. There are two holes punched in the stern. They are each large enough that I could crawl through them. Workers are busy cutting and measuring. There are work benches set up on the dock with stacks of lumber near them.

I say, "Those holes aren't all that big. I would think it would take only a day or so to cut the lumber to cover them up."

"They can't just pound new boards in," Jade replies. "They have to be fitted and caulked so that they won't leak. It takes time for each small section to be measured properly, the lumber cut to specifications, and then put into place and sealed."

The ship doesn't seem large enough to me to fit two humans, a couple trolls, an elf, and five ogres. "Are we all going to fit on this ship?"

Jade nods. "The Horn is designed to be a cargo ship. We won't have much in the way of goods, so yes, there will be plenty of room. We'll string hammocks in the hold. Chortnel and Grain will stay with me in my cabin."

"Why them?"

"Because they are female."

"Flavor is female."

"I know, but between Chortnel and Flavor, I will only have room for one. Chortnel is the smaller of the two, and I'm thinking Flavor will want to stay with her garden anyway."

I can't argue with that logic. We walk back to town and spend the rest of the day learning about Harbortown or playing with Sam. Halle goes fishing in a small rowboat with one of the sprites working for the Yeos.

The weather is good today. Mostly blue skies with puffy white clouds stacked up here and there towards the horizon. A good omen, but I should know better. My luck has not been great these last few months.

In the town commons, the clock looms over everything. The month counter is at three now and the day is twenty-two. Funny how my memories feel like both ancient history and yesterday's events.

The next day, we relax. I go out fishing and take Sam with me. I catch a couple salmon and let Sam have them. Halle gets impatient waiting for Chortnel to catch something and dives in the water. She chases the fish off and no one else catches anything, so we row back to shore.

Dinner is quiet. I think about going out to the tunnel entrance tonight. Maybe everyone is.

When it gets dark, we meet on the docks. Paul has boats and rowers waiting, along with a dozen archers. Since there really is no need for them, my companions see us off, then remain behind.

Chortnel hugs me, then Jade. "Be safe, both of you. You are too precious to lose out there."

I say, "I've survived worse, haven't I, Chortnel?" I grin at her and lift my staff to get in one of the boats. Jade gets into one of the others, then we are off. Each boat has a sprite on the tiller. Apparently, they see well with just the dome night lights.

We are quiet as we peer into the darkness once we round the channel's end and head for the tunnel. We are a kilometer away when two of the sprites sound an alarm. The one on our boat points towards the rocky beach protecting Seacove.

There's a flash, then a whistle. Something splashes in front of us, but far enough I don't get sprayed.

The tiller person says, "There are five boats. Three have archers in them, two have the guns mounted."

Another flash and whistle, and a large splash erupts near Jade's boat. I can't see where the boats are except for the cannon flash, but I stand and raise my staff. I think I can send light in that direction so we can all see what we are aiming at. The tip of my staff glows and gets brighter. Then I send energy towards the area where the flashes came from but up a little so everything in the area will be lit up.

As soon as I let the energy go, I'm hit with arrows. Three painful shocks, and I cry out. My staff drops into the water and I fall back. One of the archers catches me and checks the penetrations. I look down and there's an arrow in my right shoulder. My hand feels numb. There's another in my chest, and it hurts worse than the collar when I try to breath. The last one has pierced my lower gut area. It's bleeding pretty good down there. I grit my teeth and say, "Please, make sure you get my staff out of the water."

The archer looks around. "I don't see it." He calls to the sprite. "Can you see Hawk's staff in the water anywhere?"

The sprite is turning the boat to face the bow towards the enemy. They look into the water around us. "No, it's nowhere around the boat. Maybe it sunk."

The sprite then says, "You were hit bad. I'll turn us around and head back to the docks."

I say, "No, you make sure they others are safe. I can hold on long enough to make sure we all get back in one piece."

The sprite shakes its head. "I think your lights were enough to do the trick. Jade has used the wind to blow them back towards the rocks. They are going to be busy for a while avoiding crashing into them. The other two boats can go meet the dwarves. You're bleeding a lot. We need to get you to a healer right away."

I bite my lip as the pain continues to wash over me. "Alright, if she has it under control, then take me back."

The ride back is mostly smooth, but every wave jars the arrows sticking out of me. I mutter, "Can someone take these damn arrows out?"

One of the archers says, "No, you might bleed out. Best if we leave them where they are until we can get you to the healer."

The sprite doesn't bother going around to the docks. She beaches the boat, which makes me grit my teeth at the sudden stop. Two of the archers pick me up, and two more jump over the side. They turn and reach for me and bring me down as slowly as they can. It's not as painful as it was right after being hit, but I start to lose focus. Shivering, I ask, "Why is it so cold?" Then I pass out.

I'd think that waking up after blacking out would get easier, with all the times it's happened to me. But no. My head hurts, and this time there are other places on my body that are painful. I groan.

"Shh now," someone says, "you need to lie still and let the poultices heal you."

The voice doesn't belong to Grain. I open my eyes and see a ceiling. I try to sit up, but using my muscles causes me more pain.

I ask, "What happened?"

"You were shot with three arrows. Nearly lost you when you came in two days ago."

I've been I bed for two days? How can that be? I remember standing up to shoot light at the pirate boats and then... pain.

"Did anyone else get hurt?" I ask.

Chortnel comes into view. She says, "No, your magic fire light worked. It showed us where the pirates were, and Jade pushed them onto the rocks."

"What about Sparks?"

Chortnel said, "He wasn't with them."

"The dwarves? Did the dwarves come from Fuutenhold?"

"Yes, they're here. We've been talking about what to do."

I sit up despite the pain. It makes me gasp, and I have to take a couple slow deep breaths before speaking. An elf is at my side. He says. "You need to lie down to make the medicine work. You've lost a lot of blood and you need to heal."

I say, "Can't you just put your hands on me and heal the wounds?"

The healer says, "We did that. Your friend Grain exhausted herself saving you. The only reason she's not here now is she was falling asleep on her feet."

I try to sit up. "We need to go after them. Enough playing around. Just get me my staff and…"

Chortnel says, "Your staff is lost."

I remember now that when I'd been hit with the arrows, I'd lost my grip on the staff and it had fallen. "Did you look for it?"

Chortnel says, "Hawk, I've been back to that spot three times in the last two days. Halle and I have dived and looked. It's nowhere to be found."

I look at the healer. "Can I move without opening up the wounds?"

The healer says, "I can keep your wounds healed, but you are weak from the loss of blood. You need to eat and sleep for a few days before attempting to do anything."

I look around. "Where are the others?"

Chortnel says, "In a meeting, discussing what we can do against Sparks and his cannon boats."

I slowly stand up, and the room whirls around me. I reach out and grab Chortnel. "Take me to the meeting. I'm going to end this, staff or no staff."

Chortnel says, "You're too weak, Hawk."

I yell, "I don't care! Take me to the meeting!"

Then the room starts whirling around me and I black out again.

Chapter Thirty-One

The Pirate Solution

When I awake this time, I'm feeling a little better. I sit up in bed. Grain is sleeping in a chair next to me.

I swing my legs around and sit up. There's no dizziness, but the wounds in my shoulder, chest, and gut hurt. I have to pee. There's a chamber pot near the bed and I use it, sighing with relief. When I'm done, I turn and see that Grain is awake.

"You shouldn't be standing up yet."

I say, "I feel much better, I hope you didn't overtax yourself healing me."

Grain stretches and then stands. "I did what needed to be done. I'll get you some food. You'll need it." She turns to leave.

I say, "Grain?" She stops and looks at me. "I want you to know, I am very grateful for your friendship."

She smiles at me, looking into my eyes. "I left my home to find someone to keep the Dome from failing. I believe you are that someone, Hawk. I will do whatever needs doing to help you on your quest." Then she leaves.

I'm not so sure any more about the quest. It doesn't seem to be leading us anywhere towards fixing the Dome. I have powers, but how am I supposed to use them? What can Jade do by controlling the wind? The Dome falling apart is far too big of a problem for a couple of young humans to fix.

I sit on the bed. Chortnel, Halle, the ogres, and Sam come in. Sam runs to me with a bark and licks my hands and face as I bend down to give him a hug. When he has settled down next to me, I look at Chortnel and Flavor and remember to ask what I had forgotten to ask Grain.

"How long was I out this time?"

Chortnel says, "Just a day."

"Is Jade's ship repaired?"

"She's there now inspecting it. She says we should be able to leave tomorrow."

I say, "So, what are we going to do about the pirates?"

Flavor says, "We decided to attack tonight. We go up the channel, then Jade will use wind on the archers."

I have an idea. "I want to go in from the hidden cove entrance."

Chortnel says, "We can't land boats there. It's too rocky."

I say, "But under the rocks is sand, right?"

Chortnel thinks about this. "Yes, they are lying on a beach of sand, but what does that matter?"

"I'll use the power to blow them out. I'll get rid of all the rocks so the boats can land on the beach."

Chortnel says, "They will hear us coming and come to defend."

"I'm counting on that. We will force them to fight us from two positions. Sparks won't have a plan for dealing with a force coming from that direction."

Chortnel and Flavor rub their chins. Flavor says, "We take a boat of archers who are good with the sword, plus my garden and me. Yes, I think that might work, Hawk Archer."

Grain returns with a bowl of the fish stew for me.

"Thank you, Grain," I say. "I'm going to miss this soup when we leave."

Grain says, "No you won't. You'll most likely be sick of it after a month on the sea."

"What do you mean?"

"It's fish, broth, seaweed, and a few spices. All ingredients we will have in abundance on once we get underway. It will be the main meal until we reach land."

I dip the spoon and blow on the steaming soup before putting it in my mouth. I savor that first spoonful, then quickly take another. "I don't know, I think I could eat this for the rest of my life."

Jim and Lian Seo, Jade, and Paul Yee come in. Jade says, "After a month you will think you've had as much of that soup as you ever want for the rest of your life."

"Maybe. It beats a lot of the food I've eaten so far on this quest."

Jim says to me, "We've decided to go tonight. We will send every boat we have up the channel into Seacove. Jade will lead us and take the archers out using her wind power. Are you well enough to join us?"

"Yes, but I have a different plan." I outline my idea.

Paul says, "Are you sure you can blast enough rocks to open up the beach?"

I am confident. The power is strong enough to bring down buildings, and I've used it like that in Fuutenhold. I say, "Yes, I will have no problem getting a couple boats safely into Seacove."

"They will hear you coming."

I say, "If they get too close, they will die. I won't aim the power at them, but I won't let anyone stop me this time either. I want Mr. Sparks alive, and I won't use the power to directly kill anyone unless they are trying to kill us." Then I ask, "Where are Jasmine and her dwarves?"

"They are camped down by the beach, waiting for nightfall."

I say, "I will take Chortnel, Flavor and her garden, and a boatload of dwarves who can aim a bow and use a sword. We'll attack them on two fronts and find Mr. Sparks. I think we should also get his friend Andre. He knows how to make cannons. That makes him dangerous."

Jim says, "Already decided. We go in with the objective of capturing Sparks and Andre. The rest will be told that if they are peaceful, they can remain in Seacove, but if they commit any acts of piracy, we'll be back and will destroy the village."

I say, "I think the Mistress of Seacove, Drafa, will want to avoid that, don't you think?"

Jim says, "Drafa is not really a leader. More like an organizer. Seacove never was much of a town until Sparks went in and took over. Once Sparks is gone, the village will go back to being just a small collection of fishermen and gardeners."

"Okay," I say, "so I take a contingent around to the back, blast the rocks off the beach, and the rest of you wait just out of sight of the archers. When you hear me start blasting, you attack. Then we meet up in the middle somewhere."

I think about the last fight. "The last time they knew we were coming. What if they know about tonight's attack?"

Paul says, "We discovered a sprite was giving information to sprites from Seacove. That has been taken care of."

"Okay, then I guess we wait for the darkness."

My group of friends stays behind. The rest depart the hut. Jade says, "We'll be able to leave once this business is finished."

I smile. "I'm glad to hear that. Have you had any more visions?"

She nods. "Two while you were sleeping. They don't seem to get any stronger like the first one did."

I want to hear Jade's story, but it can wait until we're on our way across the sea. I'm feeling full and a little sleepy. "I want to take a nap. Can someone come get me when it's time?"

Chortnel says, "I will wake you when it's time to go."

The others leave the hut, and I get back on the bed, feeling a bit dizzy. I wonder if Grain or another of the healers put something in my soup. I am asleep almost before my head gets settled on my pillow.

"Hawk, time to wake up." Someone is nudging my arm. I groan and roll over. "Hawk, come on, it's time to go." I recognize Chortnel's voice and come awake. I realize what she means and sit up.

"Okay, let's go then." I swing my feet to the floor and look around. "Where are my shoes?"

Chortnel says, "They are right by your feet. Look down." I look down, but a yawn forces my eyes to close for a second. When I open them, I see my shoes neatly placed near my bed. I put my feet into them and stand up.

Chortnel says, "You might want to put on some pants, too."

I look down. I'm dressed in a sleeping gown, a simple piece of cloth with sleeves and hole for my head. I pull my feet out of the shoes, then Chortnel hands me a pile of clothing neatly folded.

"Thanks, just give me a sec."

I dress, then we move out of the hut. The rest of my friends, along with Jasmine and a dozen dwarves, are waiting. We walk to the docks, not saying anything. When we arrive, we move to the boats reserved for us.

The rest of the dwarves, along with townspeople and Jade in the front boat, are waiting for us. Their boats bob in the water just beyond the docks. We get in and set out.

I wave to Jade and she waves back, then we go in our separate directions.

The sparse light from the Dome is barely enough to make our way around the main promontory of Seacove's rocky beach. When we are close enough that I can hit the rocks with power, but far enough that nothing will blow back on us, I signal to stop.

I look around and whisper loud enough for everyone to hear. "Are we ready?"

The other boats are arrayed to the side and a bit behind me. Everyone with a bow has them at the ready.

I look back at the rocky beach and aim power. There is a huge blast, and the rubble is pushed forward up the beach. I blast again, and more rocks are disintegrated. The water rushes in to fill the gaps I'm leaving. I glance nervously at the top of the rocks, remembering the arrows that pierced me on the last outing. I decide to bring some light there.

I know the trees didn't do anything to deserve being burned, but I don't see a better way to light up the area, so I blast them and set them all on fire. In the light, I feel a little easier. I blast my way through the rocks, pulverizing them until there's a path wide enough for two boats to land side by side.

I say, "Let's go in." The archers put down their bows and take up the oars. We move closer in. I'm standing in the bow of the first boat looking for movement. It doesn't take long until I hear cannon blasts from the channel. I can only hope Jade overcame both their archers and those cannons.

There's another cannon blast, and I notice movement beyond the fire. I hear arrows hissing by us and plopping into the water. I don't hesitate. I aim power where I see the movement, and three men with bows go flying backwards in the air.

The boat crunches to a halt, and I nearly go flying into the water.

"We must have hit an underwater boulder," I say.

Someone says, "Try to maneuver around it."

We're about ten meters from the beach. I say, "Close enough." I jump into the water and reach for the bottom with my feet. It's there, but the water is up to my chin. I feel around for the bow and pull it off the rock and try to guide it up to the beach. More arrows whiz down on us. I hear someone cry in pain.

I turn around and send another blast of power. There's an explosion, and people again go flying. I climb out of the water and begin walking towards the village. I don't hesitate. At any movement, I blast away. I can see people running away from me now.

I yell at the top of my lungs, "If you want me to stop, bring me Mr. Sparks. I won't harm anyone, but I won't hold back until he's given up to me."

I don't hear anything from the village and continue walking. My companions catch up to me and we enter the village. It's quiet and there's no movement. I'm not in the mood for waiting.

I say, "I'm going to start blasting buildings. If you are inside, you most likely will be hurt or killed. You have until the count of five to get out."

I start counting backwards. I can hear people scuffling in some of the buildings. I yell, "Five." A door opens.

"Four." People run out and away from us.

"Three." More doors open, more people pour out.

"Two." I raise my hands.

"One." I send power into the nearest building, and my blast takes out the center of it, sending splinters and pieces of wood up into the sky. I send a broader blast to keep the debris from hitting us.

A voice calls out, "Okay, we'll give you Sparks!"

I say, "I want Andre as well. Bring them both here or I'll keep blowing up your village."

Men come out into the light of the burning buildings and trees. They are holding Mr. Sparks, his hands bound. He is dressed in a night gown and his feet are bare.

"Here's Sparks," one of the men says. "We don't know where Andre is."

I notice the cannons are silent, and then I notice the other contingent with Jade in the lead walking towards us. They are holding Andre, his hands bound as well.

It's over. The pirates are defeated.

Chapter Thirty-Two

The Departure

Drafa paces back and forth in front of the assembled tribune. Chortnel tells me that is how sprites show anger. Drafa must be very angry. Every so often, she stops pacing and throws an angry grimace my way.

Jade, Chortnel, Grain, and Flavor are sitting in the audience with me for the sentencing. Jade and I had been offered a seat on the judge's panel to decide the fate of Mr. Sparks, his friend Andre, and the pirates who had participated in killing dwarves. We turned it down. It is over as far as I am concerned.

Jade was busy making sure everything was ready for us to depart. She hadn't wanted to be at this meeting, but I told her she was important to it, so she agreed to come.

Drafa says, "It's outrageous that you come to my village and destroy it like that. I demand compensation and punishment for those who carried it out." She points a finger directly at me. I feel indifferent. There is no way these people are going to lock me up or sanction me. The only thing they might do is banish me, which will work well with our current plans.

But the tribunal decided it would be good politics to hear Drafa out and perhaps offer some sort of payment. Seacove might not be the threat it had been, but good relations there means less friction and a possible end to the fighting between the two settlements. Many of the sprites have relatives in both towns.

Jim stands up. "I understand your anger, Drafa, and I assure you we intend to offer you aid in helping to repair any damage. But you must also understand that you sheltered a criminal who was determined to destroy Harbortown. That can't be overlooked." He sits.

Drafa stops long enough to bang a fist on the table. "I did not attack Harbortown. I did not set your buildings on fire or blow up your beach. I demand the criminal who did this be turned over to me for trial and punishment."

Tian stands and addresses Drafa. "You demand responsibility from others but take none yourself. We all know you profited from Mr. Spark's presence. You did nothing to stop him when he attacked us and the dwarves. You stood by while his cannons were mounted on boats stolen from the dwarves, and then were used against us and the dwarves of Fuutenhold. I am willing to be a good neighbor and help Seacove recover." She takes a deep breath, then comes around the table and stands in front of Drafa. "But know this, good woman. It is only our kindness and sense of being good neighbors that prevents us from taking you into custody and throwing you in the brig with your friends Sparks and Andre."

Drafa stops, mouth gaping, trying to say something, but no words come out.

Tian gives her a sunny smile. "Now, I suggest you go back to Seacove and make a list of what you need in the way of materials and labor. Please send it to me directly and I will personally see that it is taken care of." She returns to her seat and before sitting down adds, "You are dismissed."

Drafa lets out a strangled sound as two dwarves flank her and lead her from the room.

Jim says, "Bring in the prisoners."

A different door opens, and guards come in, holding the arms of Mr. Sparks and Andre. Their hands are bound in front of them, and their legs are tied such that they have to shuffle in. When they stand before the Tribune, Jim says, "You have been found guilty of murder, destruction of property, and theft. Do you have any last words before we pronounce your sentence?"

Mr. Sparks grins at him. "Begging your pardon, sir and lady, but might I ask for just a tiny favor before I give you a speech?"

Jim looks at the rest of the judges. No one seems inclined to deny Sparks. He says, "Very well, what is it you want?"

"Nothing, nothing at all. Just a word if you will. Just a small chat with Mr. Archer if you don't mind."

Jim looks surprised. "Why would you want to talk with Hawk?"

I want to second that with my own question, but I wait for Spark's answer. "If you will indulge a poor old sod," Sparks says, "I'd like to discuss a topic of mutual benefit to Mr. Archer and myself." He looks at me with a hopeful expression.

Jim says, "If Hawk agrees, it's fine by me, but you will remain in your ropes. No tricks from you, or the sentence will be lethal and quick. Do you understand?"

"I certainly do, judge! I understand completely." He turns to me. "Mr. Archer, if you please. I assure you that you want to hear me out."

I'm curious and so inclined to agree. "As long as my friends come with us. Let's go to the outer room." Chortnel and the others nod assent, then two of the guards take Mr. Sparks to the door he was led in from. We follow along.

When we are in the waiting room beyond the door, Sparks turns to me. "I understand you feeling a little animosity toward me, Mr. Archer. I am sorry for all that's happened between us."

"Get to the point."

Mr. Sparks sighs. "The world would be such a better place if people acted with politeness and civility, don't you think Mr. Archer?"

"You tried to kill me and my friends. I'm not feeling very polite when it comes to you, Sparks. What is it you want?"

Sparks eyes get that mean gleam even while his mouth stays formed in the guileless smile he's so good at. "Right you are, Mr. Archer. There's a whole room waiting for us, after all. I'll get right to the point then." He takes a breath and says, "I couldn't help notice that you had a staff when I saw you across the lines of fighting."

I nod. "I did have one, yes."

"And you lost it somehow?"

"I lost it when your archers put arrows in me."

Sparks nods. "Yes, regrettable that. Tsk tsk. I am glad you survived that misunderstanding, Mr. Archer. But I also noticed the degree of control you showed while using the staff was missing in your second attack. I think that staff is very important to you, is it not?"

"Yes."

Sparks clears his throat. "Have you tried replacing it?"

Now I'm suspicious. Why does he want to know this? Does he think he can use me somehow if I have the staff?

Chortnel says, "We've tried, and nothing used works nearly as well as that staff."

Sparks nods. "Yes, I thought that might be the case. You see, when I saw you with that staff, I thought it was remarkable. You held a piece of white yew in your hands, and none of that is available for a thousand leagues of our humble villages here. If I might ask Mr. Archer, where did you happen to get it?"

"I don't see how that's important or how this is somehow going to stop the Tribune from stringing you up by your neck."

"Right. I do tend to get sidetracked when I talk, don't I? I can be downright convoluted, some tell me." He chuckles and notices I'm not amused. "Right, well it's like this, Mr. Archer. I can help you replace your white yew staff. I know where those trees grow you know."

I'm interested now. I've tried various types of wood, and none can hold the power like my white staff did. I even tried black iron, brass, and other metals. Everything I tried melted or was reduced to splinters.

"Where do they grow?"

Sparks says, "In the forests near the village of my birth. I can guide us there if you like, then you can find a ready replacement."

I weigh the options. I had hoped to find another piece of driftwood like the one Chortnel found, but Chortnel, Grain, and the ogres helped me search and none were found.

Channeling my power rather than just throwing raw energy would be so much more beneficial to our cause. But this is a criminal who has no sense of morality and would just as soon see me dead if it meant something in it for him.

I look to Chortnel, Grain, Jade, and the others. "What do you think?"

Jade says, "I can't believe you are considering this. He's a murderer. Having him on my ship is the same as bringing one of those dwarven exploding metal things on board. It could go off at any time."

Sparks says, "I promise you Captain Jade, I will remain quiet and meek as a mouse. There will be no trouble from me or my friend Andre, I assure you."

Jade turns to him. "Why should I agree to bringing Andre! I'm having trouble with the idea of you on my ship by yourself, let alone your murdering partner."

Spark says, "I realize Andre and I have created this animosity. It is completely our fault for having such hubris as to think we could take your ship from you. But if you have an ounce of compassion and pity, won't you consider poor old Mr. Sparks' situation? How can I live with myself if I escape death, only to leave my special Andre to hang without me?"

He clasps his hands and even sinks to his knees. "Please, I beg you, Captain. Have pity on us. I give you my solemn word I will be of no problem to you. I will do your bidding the whole trip. I have experience on board a ship like yours, as does Andre. We can be of use to you."

I look at Chortnel. "What do you think?"

Chortnel says, "It's been your quest from the start, Hawk, and now it looks like it will be Jade's as well. My opinion is that if you can find a replacement for your staff, we will all greatly benefit. The risk of taking this... person with us is worth it, I think. Remember, Mr. Sparks didn't treat us like slaves, but like companions. You were willing to remain as a pirate until things got bad. I say we try to get the council to banish them both, and let's go get you another staff."

We return, and I ask the council to replace execution with banishment. They are reluctant at first, but killing people isn't something that sits lightly with any right-thinking person, even if it's just punishment. They agree that as long as Sparks and Andre never return to their harbor, we can take custody of them.

The loyal pirates are given sentences of labor to the council for three years. They will be kept locked up while not working and put in restraints so they can't escape while they are. I take custody of Mr. Sparks and Andre.

I ask Jade, "Are we ready to leave?"

She nods. "The ship is in dock, loaded with supplies and ready to sail."

"Then let's say our goodbyes and get going."

I approach the Seos. "We are ready to go. I just wanted to thank you both and your town for your help."

Jim says, "You have helped us, Hawk Archer. We wish you all safe journeys." He grasps my arm, and we hold for a few seconds. Then he does the same with each member of the party. With Sam, he gets on one knee and offers him a snack. Sam sniffs and then takes it. Jim pats his head. "I am going to miss you, Sam. You be sure to take care of Hawk and the others."

Tian comes and hugs each of us. "I wish you all great success in your quest. You are all welcome back here if you come this way."

We take our leave and walk to the docks. No one has much to say, not even Sparks, who normally can't be persuaded to shut up. When we get to the ship, I lead the two prisoners on board. Two of the ogres remain to untie the lines, and Jade gives orders to the other ogres to set the sail. Apparently, she has been training them over the last two days.

Two oar boats are tied to the ship with thick ropes. When the ogres are on board, Jade signals them to pull us out of the harbor. I wave to those on the dock.

When we are in open water, Jade has the boats maneuver us to face the horizon. I stand on the deck at the stern and continue waving goodbye. I want to give them something to remember me by, so I aim power up into the sky over their heads and release it. There is a loud boom and a flash of light.

Those on the dock cheer and wave until I can no longer see them. I make my way to the bow and look towards where we are headed. When the sails are filled and we are underway, Jade comes to stand next to me.

She says, "We need to get one thing straight, Hawk."

I ask, "What is that?"

She replies, "You've been in charge of this quest up to now, but this is my ship. Until we are back on land, I'm the one in charge. Agreed?"

I smile and take her hand. "Of course, captain. You are in charge."

We stand there for a while, holding hands and looking towards the horizon. I ponder our destiny and what adventures are to come.

The End.

Printed in Great Britain
by Amazon